"Nancy Lavo does it again! *The Perfect Getaway* will draw you in from the very first line. Memorable characters plus a heart-thumping plot equal a feel-good read you won't be able to put down. *The Perfect Getaway* will make you miss all the great people of Village Green and leave you wanting to visit again real soon."

—Kelley Rene,
award-winning author of *Kamilah*,
*Saving Sabine*, and *Romanian Runaway*

"*The Perfect Get Away* by Nancy Lavo will make you smile long after you close the book. Lavo writes romance in the style of Lisa Wingate's *Blue Moon Bay* and *Firefly Island*, with unforgettable characters, lighthearted banter, and a touch of intrigue."

—Peggy Purser Freeman,
author and inspirational speaker

"Once again, Nancy Lavo has crafted a charming story of small-town Texas life that's impossible to put down! *The Perfect Getaway* is a delightful escape from the mundane, with its swoony, slow-build romance, multigenerational friendships, and peek-over-your shoulder suspense. And did I mention funny? *The Perfect Getaway* sparkles with humor and tenderness. Nancy Lavo is a master storyteller!"

—Teresa G. Wells, author and former librarian

LONE STAR LOVES

# The Perfect Getaway

BOOK 3

NANCY LAVO

Birmingham, Alabama

The Perfect Getaway

Iron Stream Fiction
An imprint of Iron Stream Media
100 Missionary Ridge
Birmingham, AL 35242
IronStreamMedia.com

Library of Congress Control Number: 2023936760

Cover design by For the Muse Designs

ISBN: 978-1-56309-641-9 (paperback)
ISBN: 978-1-56309-642-6 (eBook)

1 2 3 4 5—28 27 26 25 24

# DEDICATION

To my husband, John. I'm so very glad I get to do life with you.

# ACKNOWLEDGMENTS

Publishing a book is a team effort. Many, many thanks to Susan Cornell, Michele Trumble, Kim McCulla, and the wonderful team at Iron Stream Media. Your hard work and attention to detail make every book shine. It's an honor to work with you.

I'm so grateful for my critique group. What a privilege to work with these wise and supportive women.

My agent, Tamela Hancock Murray, is a fountain of knowledge and encouragement. I'm blessed to have her in my corner.

A big thank you to my family for their love and encouragement.

Finally, thank you, readers, for letting me share my stories with you. I appreciate your kind support more than you know. Keep in touch by visiting my website at www.nancylavo.com.

# CHAPTER ONE

Riley Vreeland moved stealthily through the darkened house, fearful any sudden noise or movement would alert him to her intentions. Ridiculous, since he lived several miles away and no doubt slept at this ungodly hour, but reasonable or not, she kept looking over her shoulder, wondering when he would next appear.

She rolled her two large suitcases into the garage and hefted them into the back of her SUV, stuffing them in between stacks of plastic storage bins filled with school supplies and boxes of photos and mementos. It would be easier to pack with her vehicle in the driveway, but she couldn't risk the exposure.

If Ron discovered her plans, she'd never get away.

She lowered the hatchback and latched it, jumping at the loud click when the mechanism engaged. Frozen, she waited, listening hard into the silence, half expecting to hear his car pull up in the driveway on the other side of the door.

The only sound was the thundering of her heart.

Riley reentered the house, making one more pass through to be certain she'd turned everything off. She told herself she'd be back as soon as she was free of him, though whether she'd live again in her childhood home or put it on the market remained up in the air.

She walked through each room, breathing in a hundred sweet memories of the wonderful life she'd shared here with her parents.

She paused at the door of their room, the queen-sized bed made up as if in expectation of their return. Tears from a seemingly endless supply clouded her vision.

At this moment, she was glad they were gone, safe in the arms of Jesus, undisturbed by the nightmarish turn in her life. She rubbed a hand over her heart. Sometimes she missed them so much it hurt. The sudden loss of their presence and wisdom left a gaping hole, and when this was behind her, she promised to take the time to honor their memory and grieve them properly.

For now, she focused on escape.

Every light was off, every ceiling fan stilled, the air conditioner shut down. She'd given a key to their longtime neighbors, asking them to check on the house periodically until she returned. She'd told them she'd be traveling for the next few months with no set itinerary and would call them every couple of weeks to be certain all was well.

Ron had never met the elderly couple, didn't know about their close association with Riley's family, but she didn't share her true plans with them, just in case. She knew from experience he could charm his way past defenses, insinuating himself into lives and secrets without anyone being aware. She'd gone to too much trouble covering her tracks to let an unsuspecting friend or neighbor give her away.

Time to go.

With one final look over her shoulder, she climbed into the SUV, her hand hesitating over the garage door opener. She swallowed past the ever-present fear. Almost there. Freedom was in her sights. *Please God, don't let him be standing in the driveway when the door goes up.*

Rolling her shoulders against the paralyzing tension, she took a deep breath and pressed the button. Her heart hammered as the door slowly rattled its way up the track. The driveway was empty.

She swallowed a cheer of pure relief. Right now she needed to stay focused. She had a lot more miles to go before she could celebrate.

The miles—and hours—passed quickly and Riley approached the sign welcoming her to Village Green a little past three in the afternoon. She'd made good time, even with the stop at the dealership just over the Texas border where she'd traded in her SUV on a new model. Before exiting the two-lane highway and pulling into town, she checked her rearview mirror for the millionth time, a particularly irrational act since, even if she was being followed, no one would think to look for her in a shiny new white vehicle with paper tags.

She looked forward to the day when she returned to her rational self.

Turning on Main Street, she slowed to the posted speed of thirty miles per hour. The aged, red-brick, two-story buildings lining the road looked like those of a dozen other little towns between Oklahoma and here. She'd passed through similar places all day, hundred-year-old small towns long past their prime, struggling to survive as jobs and opportunities moved to the big cities.

Village Green did a better job than most in masking the decay. The wood trim on the buildings looked freshly painted, and the windows in the mostly empty stores shone in the early August sun. Huge cement pots spilling over with orange and yellow blooms dotted the sidewalks that ran in front of the shops. Across the street, a couple braved the triple digit heat to sit on a shaded bench in a pretty little green space.

Small-town America. With its limited employment, housing, and amenities, nondescript Village Green was the last place someone would choose to settle.

And if God was listening, the very last place Ron would come looking.

Her map app told her to take the first right past the park. Half a block on the left was the place where she'd pick up her keys, and a block past that would be her new home. She pulled up in the driveway of the first address, belonging to Mrs. Piermont, a friend of the homeowner Riley was renting from. She shut off the engine and, after a careful sweep of the street, climbed out of the vehicle.

Mrs. Piermont's home was a showplace, a large, white, two-story home in immaculate condition, situated on a wide green lot and shaded by huge old trees. Although in the same neighborhood, Riley knew from the pictures she had seen, her more modest rental house had a smaller yard.

The smiling, grandmotherly woman who answered the door wore a chic summery pink shift with matching sandals. "You must be Riley. I'm Mary Jo. Won't you come in?"

"Thank you." After a glance over her shoulder, probably the third since she left her car, she followed her hostess along beautiful hardwood floors to a huge, obviously updated kitchen.

"Please, sit down." Mary Jo motioned toward the table. "I made some peach tea. Would you care for a glass?"

Though eager to see her new home, Riley appreciated the old-fashioned civility that made even a simple business transaction into a social event. Mary Jo would fit right in with her parents' crowd. "I'd love some. Thanks."

She let her gaze travel the light-filled room. "Your home is lovely."

"Thank you." Mary Jo carried two tall glasses of iced tea and a couple of long-handled spoons to the table. She handed one of each to Riley and sat opposite her. She slid a pretty china bowl with an assortment of sweeteners toward her. "I think you'll be pleased with the house you're renting. The Coopers have remodeled the entire place over the last couple of years. They were planning on retiring there."

"I hope they still can." Riley dumped two packets of sugar into her glass and stirred. "If they caught the cancer early enough, Mrs. Cooper can enjoy a long, healthy retirement."

The older woman beamed. "I like your positive thinking. I believe the treatment will be successful, but I have a feeling once it's finished, they'll want to stay in Houston near their daughter. As we get older, having family close by is such a comfort. Do I remember correctly that you are moving here from Oklahoma?"

"Yes, ma'am."

"Did you leave someone behind?"

Riley choked on her tea. "Oh, uh, no. It was just my parents and me. And they're both deceased."

"I'm so sorry, dear. That can be very lonely." Her expression brightened. "As beautiful as you are, I predict it won't be long before you have all the company you want with the local gentlemen buzzing around you."

Riley shuddered involuntarily. "I hope not. I've just esc—uh, ended a relationship, and I'm not looking for another one."

Mary Jo's wise blue eyes studied her for a moment. "Then you're smart to take a break." She got up from the table and picked up a large envelope off the counter and handed it to her. "The Coopers left this packet for you with the keys to the house and instructions about the sprinkler system and appliances. Since I knew you were coming, I went in this morning and turned down the air conditioner."

"Thank you." Riley placed it on the table. "Do you happen to know if the Coopers have a security system in their home?"

Mary Jo smiled and shook her head. "Other than the bank, I doubt there's a security system in the entire town. Village Green is pretty small. We don't have a lot of crime."

"That's good to know." She finished the rest of her drink, picked up the packet, and stood. "Thank you so much for the tea. I think I'll head over to the house and get everything unloaded before it gets dark."

"Can I help you?"

"No thanks. It's not that much."

Her hostess stood as well. "Let me give you my telephone number in case you change your mind." She picked up a pen and wrote her name and number on a sheet of paper. "May I get your number as well? I promise I won't annoy you with calls, but I think it's important for people who live alone to have someone looking out for them."

How many times had her mother said the same thing? Riley wrote her name and her father's cell phone number on the pad of paper, since she'd discontinued the service on her own phone.

Mary Jo walked her to the front door. Hand on the knob, she paused to look her in the eye. "May I ask you a personal question?"

Riley tensed as she nodded.

"Are you a believer?"

Her expression relaxed into a smile. "Yes, ma'am."

Mary Jo grinned. "I'm so glad. In times of upheaval, like a move or new job, it's especially comforting to know the Lord is our refuge and strength, a very present help in trouble."

Riley blinked back a threatening tear. Psalm 46:1 was one of her father's favorite verses. "Thank you. I needed the reminder today."

Mary Jo swung the door open. "I'd like to call you in a day or two to see how you're settling in, if that's okay?"

"Yes, ma'am, I'd like that."

★     ★     ★

Sam answered his cell phone on the first ring. "Hey, Mary Jo! What's up?"

"Do you have a minute, dear one?"

He steered the squad car to the side of the road and shifted into park. "Absolutely. What can I do for you?"

"The young woman who's renting the Coopers' place and taking over for Elizabeth at the school just stopped by to pick up the keys, and she seemed a little . . . off."

"How so?"

"She kept checking the street in front of my house, as if she were looking for someone. This is going to sound silly, but it appeared to me that she thought she was being followed."

"That's weird."

"Then she asked me if the Coopers' house had a security system."

He snorted. "In Village Green?"

"Exactly. I assured her we have very little crime here, but she still seemed . . . I don't know . . . on edge. I thought if you had a minute, you could stop over there and introduce yourself. Maybe if she knew law enforcement was close by, she could relax a little."

"I'm four blocks away. I can be at her place in five minutes."

"I would appreciate it. And I hope you'll stop by for breakfast one day this week. We'll have pancakes and catch up."

"Sounds great."

"Any day is fine with me. And thank you for looking in at the Coopers'."

"No problem. What's the renter's name?"

"Riley Vreeland. You probably shouldn't mention I told you she looked nervous. She might not appreciate my interference."

He chuckled. "I won't say a word."

He pulled back out onto the road, this time heading in the direction of the Cooper place. In no time, he was cruising the tree-lined street. Up ahead, a woman with her back to him stood in the driveway, at the raised hatch of a late model SUV.

He radioed in his position, parked at the curb, and climbed out of the patrol car. "Hello? Ms. Vreeland?"

At his call, the woman turned, took one look at him, and dropped the plastic box she held. Her face went white, her mouth slack, her wide eyes the only spots of color on her face. When she swayed, he closed the short distance between them at a run.

"Oh, hey, don't do that." He caught her upper arm and gently lowered her to the driveway. "Put your head down and breathe slowly."

He knelt beside her, guiding her to the recovery position with gentle pressure on her back. "That's good. Breathe. Slow and easy."

After four or five long breaths, she pushed up against his hand into a seated position. "How did you—" She stopped with a guilty grimace. "Why are you here?"

Remaining at her level, he eased back into a crouch. "Mary Jo called and told me you were moving in. I was in the neighborhood, so I figured I'd stop by and see if you could use some help."

"Oh."

He grinned. "You know, as a cop, I get a lot of different reactions from people, but I can honestly say this is the first time I've had someone swoon. You got a thing for men in uniform?"

Her weak attempt to smile at his joke was accompanied by a rush of color. "I don't know what that was."

It looked like stark terror to him. "Probably the heat. Let's get you out of the sun, and I'll fix you a glass of water."

"No." Her voice and head shake were firm. "I've got a bottle of water inside."

"Fine. You go in, and I'll pick up this stuff off the driveway."

Another shake of her head. "I can take care of it."

"Let me help you. It's my job." He tried another grin. "You know, *serve* and protect. I won't stay."

That seemed to calm her. "Okay."

He helped her to her feet, then watched her walk up the front sidewalk. She stopped twice to turn around and check his position before continuing into the house. She seemed nervous but steady. No danger of keeling over.

He bent to pick up the scattered contents from the now cracked bin, dozens of colorful laminated pictures of animals and their corresponding letters—clearly classroom supplies—and return them to the container. Pin holes in the corners said this wasn't the first time she'd used the illustrations. So Mary Jo's nervous friend wasn't new to the classroom. He fitted the lid on the box and carried it to the front door, arriving there at the same time she did.

She seemed to have trouble meeting his eyes as she pushed open the glass storm door and extended her hands. "I'll take it from here."

"Just show me where you want it, and I'll put it there." He could see an argument coming. "It's okay. I'm one of the good guys." When she met his gaze with a wary one, he smiled and nodded. "Really."

She paused, scanning his face and apparently weighing her options. Her shoulders sagged slightly. "This way."

She led him through the living room and down the hall, stopping at the first bedroom. "If you'll just put it there, that'll be great."

"No problem." He placed the box on the floor in the corner. "I'll go get the rest."

She shook her head. "That's okay. I've got it."

No way he was leaving until he figured out why she wanted so badly to be rid of him. He gave her face a quick study. "Your color is better, but I don't think we should take any chances with the heat. I'll unload the rest of the stuff into the house, and you can take it from there."

She huffed out a frustrated breath. "I can handle it."

"I'm sure you're more than competent, but I'd like to help. Humor me. We good guys like to feel useful."

"Fine."

Perspiration ran in sticky rivulets down his face and dampened the heavy fabric of his uniform a half an hour later as he carried in the last few items. He brushed the top of his sleeve across his face. "Hot work."

"I appreciate you carrying it all inside." In an obvious effort to herd him out, she walked toward the door as she spoke.

Instead of following her lead, he detoured toward the kitchen. "Can I grab a glass of water before I go? My shift isn't over for a couple more hours, and I'm pretty parched."

A look of frustration passed over her face, but it spoke to him of innate kindness when she followed him into the kitchen though she clearly wanted him gone. She stopped in the center of the room, two fingers to her lips, considering the wall of cabinets.

"Glasses are in the one next to the sink." To demonstrate, he walked over, opened the door, and pulled out a glass.

Her brows lifted. "You've been here before?"

He grinned. "Dozens of times. Mrs. Cooper was my first-grade teacher, and her husband was my Boy Scout leader for years." He helped himself to some ice from the freezer and filled his glass from the dispenser in the refrigerator door. Belatedly, he looked over his shoulder. "You want a drink?"

A small but genuine smile, the first he'd seen, turned up the corners of her very pretty mouth as the ridiculousness of the situation struck home. "No thanks. I'm good."

Standing face-to-face, he took the opportunity to study her over the rim of his glass. Tough to guess the age of a woman, but he'd put her between twenty-five and thirty, approximately five foot three, and 120 well-toned pounds. She had an oval face and classic features, with creamy skin and an interesting shade of eyes he bet would change from green to blue, based on what she wore. They were currently green, as was her T-shirt, and framed in thick dark lashes. Her medium brown hair was pulled up in a short ponytail, and despite the frowning suspicion, she was a beauty in a fresh-faced, cheerleader sort of way.

"The Coopers are good people." He leaned casually against the counter, hoping to put her at ease. "The breast cancer diagnosis was a real shock."

"I hope they caught it early, and she gets the very best care."

Her genuine concern for a near-stranger reinforced his assessment that buried beneath a prickly layer of standoffishness was a nice person. So what had her keyed up? "Seems like I heard it's in the very early stages. They've gone to Houston to stay with their daughter because there's some great cancer treatment center there."

"I've got the house through June, so they must not be planning on returning any time soon."

He shook his head. "I doubt they'll be coming back."

Arms still folded protectively across her chest, she relaxed enough to prop against the opposite counter. "Mrs. Piermont said the same thing."

"Her husband is already retired, and Mrs. Cooper has been talking about retiring in the next couple of years. I think the cancer diagnosis sealed the deal. Once she's healthy, I imagine they'll want to stay near their daughter. It's not like there's anything holding them here." He took a long drink of the icy water. "Worked out pretty well with you taking her job and the house. I know they're thankful to have someone staying in it while they decide if they want to sell."

She glanced around the room. "I don't know what I'd have done if they hadn't offered it to me. I'd already accepted the job when I discovered there's no rental property in Village Green. I guess I could have found something in a nearby town, but I don't know the area."

"You've never been here?"

She shook her head. "I found the job online, did my interviews by video conferencing, signed the papers electronically."

He gave a low whistle. "Talk about embracing technology. It must have come as a real shock to drive in and see how small the town is."

Her ponytail swayed with another shake of her head. "I was prepared."

"How's that?"

"I'd seen an article in a travel magazine at my dentist's office touting Village Green as an idyllic small town. When I went to the city website to read more details, I found a map and photos along with the job posting for a first-grade teacher."

His brows shot up. "A random article and a visit to a website, and you're willing to pull up stakes and move?"

She lowered her gaze. "I was ready for a change."

"I'll say." Major story here. He'd bet his badge on it. "Where'd you come from?"

She paused. "Oklahoma City."

"Do you have people back there?"

He saw a flicker of something as she lifted her eyes. Nerves? Fear? She tamped it down, covered it with a weak smile. "Nobody. My parents passed away, and I'm an only child."

"Probably got friends? A boyfriend?"

Stiffening, she pushed away from the counter. "Nobody." He noted she'd lost a little of the color she'd regained. "Do you always ask so many questions?"

He shrugged. "I'm a cop. It comes with the territory."

"Have you always wanted to be a policeman?"

Nice redirection. Apparently, she didn't want to talk about herself. He usually found the quality refreshing. Today it struck him as highly suspicious. "Ever since I was a kid. How long have you been teaching?"

"Seven years."

"That long, huh?" He screwed up his face. "So what does that make you, thirty?"

Her eyes flashed. "Don't you know it's impolite to ask a woman her age?"

"Yeah." He hung his head with sham remorse. "I can't seem to help myself. Cop thing."

"I'm twenty-nine." She slanted a look at his now-empty glass. "Are you finished with your drink?"

"Are you trying to get rid of me, Ms. Vreeland?"

She met his gaze squarely. "If I am, it doesn't seem to be working."

He laughed as he placed his glass on the counter. "I'm finished."

He took three steps in the direction of the door and stopped. "You got a piece of paper? I want to give you my phone number."

An insincere smile pasted on her face, she shook her head. "I won't need it."

"You never know. Being new in a strange town, you're bound to have questions. It's nice to have the good guys on speed dial." She didn't budge, so he added an incentive. "As soon as I give it to you, I'll leave."

She moved with unflattering haste to a pad of neon sticky notes sitting on the counter, pulled one off, and handed it to him.

Accepting it with a grin, he wrote his name and two numbers and extended it to her. "I've given you the number for the police station, and my personal number. If something comes up and you need help or a friendly voice, don't hesitate to call."

"Thank you." Without looking at it, she stuck it on the tile back-splash over the built-in desk and kept walking toward the front door. "And thank you for unloading my car."

"It's new, isn't it?" He followed close behind her. "Couldn't help noticing the temporary tag. Did you know a lot of dealers make a notation at the top of the placard listing the date of purchase?" He stopped to give her a pointed look. "You've had a busy day—driving down from Oklahoma with a stop along the way to pick up a new vehicle."

Heaving a sigh, she pushed open the storm door and stepped aside. "Goodbye, Officer."

"Goodbye, Ms. Vreeland. See you soon."

He would swear he heard her mutter right before the door slammed. "Not if I see you first."

# CHAPTER TWO

School started the second week in August. By the third day, Riley found her rhythm. Inside the concrete walls of County Elementary, she could stop looking over her shoulder and focus on the twenty precious lives entrusted to her for the coming year. Her purpose grounded her. The joy and familiarity of teaching eclipsed the tension and disorientation of uprooting to a new state, new home, and new job. With students in the seats and lessons to impart, she was in the zone.

She walked along the row of metal desks, distributing a sheet of creamy manila paper to each child. "This morning, we're going to do some drawing."

She raised her voice slightly to be heard over the shifting and shuffling and chatter. "I want you to draw a picture of your family, so I can get to know you better. Once everyone is finished, you'll each have a chance to talk about what you drew."

A hand shot up in front. Olivia pushed the bridge of her pink glasses up higher on her nose. "Do you want us to just draw people, or should we draw a picture of our house too?"

Riley had tagged Olivia as a type A personality the first day of school. "Good question. You may do whatever you think will help us learn about you."

Another hand. Noah. "Can I draw my picture in markers?"

Riley shook her head. Crayons were standard issue for first graders, and they knew it. From her observations over the last few days, she knew Noah liked to test the boundaries. "No, we'll stick to crayons."

"But crayons smear." *Test boundaries and argue.*

"Yes, they do, but a little smearing is okay because only God is perfect."

The phrase, one of her father's favorites, rolled off her tongue and brought a pang to her heart. She missed him every day. Both her parents had taught at the local college, and neither had ever had a problem integrating their faith with their calling. While sensitive to the variety of religions present in the student body, they never compromised their beliefs. How blessed she'd been to have their rich example for her life—her love for God and teaching were a direct result of their influence.

"When everyone is finished, we'll take turns talking about our pictures."

"Are you going to draw one?"

Riley smiled at Adria, who already exhibited a keen interest in justice. "Yes. I'll tell my story at the end."

She sat at her desk in the front left-hand corner of the room. "Okay, let's begin."

Talking ceased as they bent their heads over their work. The only sound in the room was the scraping of crayons over the rough paper.

Riley picked up a red crayon and tapped it to her lips as she considered what she wanted to draw.

A thin, dark-haired boy in a snug cartoon character T-shirt and worn sneakers appeared at her elbow. "I'm done, Miss Vreeland."

"Wow, Chris. That was fast."

He smiled shyly and nodded. "My mom says I'm speedy."

"She's right. Let's see what you've got." Riley took the paper illustrated with two carefully drawn figures in front of a small white house.

She handed it back to him with a smile. "This is very good. I like how neatly you've drawn your people. You still have more time. Is there anything else you want to add? A pet maybe?"

He shook his head. "Nope. Pets cost too much. It's just me and my mom."

Riley remembered meeting his mother when she dropped Chris off on the first day of school. Young and dressed in a fast-food uniform, she was in a hurry to get to work but took the time to walk him to his new classroom. A woman who put her child's welfare over her own earned high marks with Riley.

"You and your mom make a great family. Since everyone else is still working, why don't you go back to your seat and wait quietly." She pulled a large, brightly illustrated book of dinosaurs off the shelf beside her desk. "Maybe you'd like to look at this while you're waiting."

His eyes widened. "Yes, ma'am. I love dinosaurs."

He clutched the book to his chest as he made his way back to his seat. He looked up, and noting she was watching, gave her a friendly wave before opening the book.

Riley glanced down at her still-blank page. The escalating sounds of squirms and whispers said she didn't have long, so she picked up the crayon and summed up her life with a couple of squiggles and short red lines.

She looked up from her paper to scan the room. "Is everyone finished?"

All heads nodded.

"Wonderful. I can't wait to hear your stories."

"I'll go first." Overachieving Olivia waved her hand in the air.

"Thank you for offering, but today we're going to go in alphabetical order by our last names." Riley turned to the boy seated at the first desk on the far left. "Justin, would you stand up and tell us about your picture?"

Justin got to his feet, his round face a fiery red. He grunted and stammered through his description, every second obvious misery. She'd chosen him to go first because as the biggest kid in the class, the kind who'd already developed a cocky swagger by age seven, she figured it would be no big deal. Wrong. Just another reminder that appearances could be deceiving.

When he finally finished, he turned a pained look in her direction, a clear plea for permission to sit down and end the suffering.

"Thank you, Justin. I need you to remain standing for one more minute." She turned to the class. "There were two things I liked about Justin's story. First, I liked hearing that he has three older brothers. I bet he's never lonely. Secondly, I liked that even though it can be a little scary to talk in front of the group, he did it anyway."

She directed her gaze to him. "Thank you, Justin, for showing us what courage looks like."

Some of the mortification eased from his face, and a small smile turned up the corners of his wide mouth.

"I'm so proud of him for having the courage to go first and lead the way for us that I think we should give him some applause." She led the clapping. "Well done, Justin."

His face colored as his classmates celebrated him, but this time it was clearly a flush of pleasure.

Noah, the boy seated behind him, stood as Justin took his seat. The ice having been broken, he was able to make it through his description with a minimum of agony.

"Thank you, Noah. I liked hearing your story. I especially like that you have two dogs and a cat. Do you help your parents care for them?"

He nodded.

"I know they appreciate it." Her gaze traveled past him to the girl seated behind him, signaling the end of his turn. "Madeline—"

"Hey wait, Miss Vreeland." Noah remained on his feet. "Didn't I show courage?"

She swallowed a laugh at the expectant look on his face and grinned. "Yes, you absolutely did." She turned to the class. "Let's give Noah a round of applause."

For the next hour, the students talked and applauded their way through their introductory pictures.

Riley had made the same assignment to her class each year since she'd first begun teaching. Her purpose was twofold. She wanted to find out as much as possible about her students, early on. Family dynamics had a definite bearing on a child's performance. In addition, their work would be a good indication of where she needed to begin instruction.

Today's reminder that everyone benefited from a cheering section was an added bonus.

Based on what she heard this morning, the families of these first graders were similar to those of her previous students in Oklahoma. Of the twenty kids, nearly half came from broken homes. Five lived in single-parent homes, and one was being raised by grandparents. She directed a silent prayer toward heaven, asking that in her classroom they would find the support and stability they needed to flourish. *And Father, would You show me if there's anything I can do to help bring balance to their lives?*

"Okay, everybody hand your artwork forward to the front of your row, and I'll collect them." She'd display them on the "Welcome Back to School" bulletin board.

"What about you, Miss Vreeland?" Olivia said. "Aren't you going to tell us about your picture?"

Riley put the stack of papers on her desk and picked up her drawing of a solitary figure standing in front of a house. The children stilled to listen as she lifted it for them to see. "I moved here from Oklahoma to teach at County Elementary School. I live alone in a wonderful house I'm renting from Mrs. Cooper."

Hands shot up all over the room.

"But Miss Vreeland, you didn't talk about your brothers and sisters."

She smiled and shook her head. "I don't have any."

"You can have one of my brothers," Justin offered.

"Don't you have a momma?"

"I had a momma and daddy, but they have both passed away." *So hard to say.* She took a steadying breath. "I am the only one left in my family."

"Are you very lonely?"

The sweet compassion of the children melted her heart. "I'm not lonely since I have you-all."

After a sharp knock on the door frame, the principal, Mrs. Peeper, popped her head in. "Good morning, Ms. Vreeland. Excuse me for interrupting. We've had a slight change in plans this morning. The air conditioner in the cafeteria isn't working, so instead of meeting there, Officer Sam will be doing the safety program in each of the first-grade classrooms."

"Okay. Sure." Officer Sam? Riley pressed her lips together. What was the name of the prying cop who'd helped her move in?

Mrs. Peeper entered, followed by a tall, uniformed officer carrying a large cardboard box.

"Officer Sam!" The class erupted into noisy cheers and greetings.

*Oh no.* Officer tall, dark, and nosey. Riley sighed. She supposed the odds were pretty good she'd run into him sometime, somewhere. After all, it was a *very* small town. But did it have to be so soon? And in her classroom?

Mrs. Peeper led him to Riley's side. "Ms. Vreeland, I'd like you to meet Sam Walker. He serves on the police force here in Village Green."

Riley gave him a quick once-over as he approached. He was good-looking in a clean-cut, aw-shucks sort of way. Tall and muscular without looking bulked up, with close-cropped, medium brown hair, wide, friendly eyes, and a ready, dimpled smile, Officer Dogooder reminded her of an oversized Boy Scout, or that superhero guy in the movies—Captain America—but without the shield and tights.

"We met when I moved in." Riley gave him a nod as she extended her hand to shake his, then immediately turned her attention to Mrs. Peeper. "He's obviously very popular with the students."

He didn't release the gentle pressure on her hand until she met his eyes. "It's because they don't have a problem recognizing I'm one of the good guys."

*Not that again.* She favored him with a cool smile, little more than a baring of teeth, and pulled her hand free.

"How do we want to proceed?" Riley directed the question to the principal.

"You can have a seat, and Officer Sam will take it from here."

Sam set his box of props on the floor in the front center of the room. "Good morning, kids. I'm here to remind you about things you can do to stay safe as we start this new school year. Who in this room wants to stay safe?"

All arms shot up.

"Great. Then you'll want to listen closely to what I say."

He pulled his black-and-white helmet from the box and held it high so everyone could see it. "Anybody know what this is?"

"It's a helmet."

Lowering his arms, he nodded. "That's right. This is the police helmet I wear when I ride my motorcycle on duty. Who knows why I wear it?"

"So you don't get shot."

He bit back a sigh. It saddened him that shooting and violence played prominently in the minds of kids, even first graders. "That's one reason. Can someone give me another?"

A timid hand appeared in the back of the room. "So you don't get bugs in your face?"

"Right." He laughed. "Nobody wants bugs in their face. There's another *very* important reason. Let me give you a hint. It has something to do with my head. Olivia, I see your hand up."

"Yes, sir. Policemen wear helmets when they ride motorcycles to protect their head in case of an accident."

"Exactly. My helmet protects my head. If I crash, it keeps me safe from injury. Bonus question. Call it out if you know the answer. What's in our heads that we need to protect?"

"Brains!"

"That's right. We need our brains to think and make good decisions. What else?"

"Eyes."

"Ears."

"A mouth."

"You've got it." He tapped the side of his head. "There's a lot of important things here we need to protect."

He pulled a smaller helmet from the box. "Anyone in here have one of these?"

All hands in the air.

Excellent. Several years ago they'd made a school-wide push to get helmets to every kid. Nice to see their efforts continued to pay off.

"What kind of activities do you wear a helmet for?"

"Riding my bike."

"Roller skating and skateboarding."

He nodded. "Pretty much any time you're on wheels is a good time to wear one."

"Cars have wheels, and you don't have to wear a helmet."

*There was always one.* "Good point, Noah. Thank you. You can leave your helmet home when you're riding in your car."

"NASCAR drivers wear helmets."

He'd forgotten just how quick first graders were. "Yeah, they do. They're going so fast, they need extra protection."

"NASCAR's cool."

"I think so too. Okay, I need a volunteer to let me borrow their head for a minute."

The class laughed. He selected a kid from the second row, waved him up. "It's Dwayne, right? Come stand by me, facing the class, and let's demonstrate the right way to wear this thing."

He placed the plastic headpiece on the kid's head and tilted it back off his forehead, straps dangling by his ears. "Is this the correct way to wear it?" He cupped a hand to his ear, inviting them to call out.

"No!"

"What did I do wrong?"

"You didn't buckle it on."

Sam nodded. "The helmet's not going to do any good if it's just resting on your head. You shift too fast or start to tip over and . . . bam!" He thumped the underside, causing it to slide off Dwayne's head and hit the floor with a crash.

He picked it up and repositioned it, this time adjusting the straps under his chin and fastening the buckle with a click. "Now it's snug on his head, and if he wipes out, the helmet isn't going anywhere, and his head is protected."

After removing it, he patted the kid on the back. "Thanks for your help, man."

"Miss Vreeland says we can clap when someone shows courage," Olivia explained as the kids applauded. "It takes courage to stand in front of the class."

"Yes, it does." He glanced at Ms. Vreeland. She'd been watching him carefully this morning, but her cool expression gave nothing away. He could tell she hadn't been too happy to see him when he walked in. For some reason she didn't like him. He grinned. *May as well give her a good one.*

"Before I leave this morning, I want to spend a minute talking about a different kind of safety. I'm going to need another volunteer." He leaned in toward the class, placed the side of his hand at the corner of his mouth and said in a loud whisper, "Do you think I should ask Miss Vreeland to help me?"

The class roared. Ms. Vreeland scowled.

"Maybe we should clap for her." He gave an exaggerated nod as he spoke. "That might give her the courage to stand here and help me."

The first graders burst into applause, forcing their clearly reluctant teacher to her feet.

He waved her to his side. "Come join me, Ms. Vreeland, so we can talk about stranger danger."

Something flashed across her face, fear maybe, as she slowly moved toward him. She stopped several feet from his side, her hands clasped in a white-knuckle grip. *Was it me or something I said?*

"Let's pretend Ms. Vreeland is a first grader here at County Elementary."

The kids laughed.

"She's pretty excited because her mom said she could ride her bike to school." He reached into his box, stirring the contents to find the adult-sized helmet. Aha! He grasped it and began pulling it out when he caught a glimpse of his volunteer out of the corner of his eye. Her arms were folded across her chest and her chin set at a mulish angle. Pretty clear she wasn't going to wear it without a fight.

A wise man knew how to pick his battles.

He straightened. "Looks like I don't have anything to fit her, so let's pretend she's wearing a very cool helmet.

"Imagine she's riding on the sidewalk when a car pulls up beside her and stops. The driver of the car, who is a stranger, rolls down the window and says, 'Hi, I'm lost. Would you give me directions to the grocery store?'" He turned to the class. "What should she do?"

"Keep riding."

"Don't stop."

"Great answers. Ms. Vreeland, can you tell me why you should just keep going?"

She nodded, directing her response to the class. "I can give you two reasons. One, children should not talk to strangers. Two, no adult would ask a child for directions. If they truly need help, they will ask another adult. It's creepy that they stopped a child."

Her answer gave him a neat segue into his next point. "But what if the stranger didn't look creepy? What if he had a nice smile and a cool car?"

"It doesn't matter what they look like. Don't stop."

"What if they had a cute puppy in the car and said you could hold it?"

She gave an animated shake of her head. "Don't stop."

He liked the way she played off his lead. They worked surprisingly well together. "What if they offered you—" He paused. "What's your favorite kind of cookie?"

"Snickerdoodles."

"One of my personal favorites. Okay, so what if the stranger offers you a whole bag of snickerdoodles?"

"Doesn't matter. Don't stop."

"But what if they said they were friends of your mom and dad?"

Just that quickly he felt the fragile connection between them break. She inhaled sharply, as though he'd hit a nerve, and for a moment, her eyes took on a hunted expression as she searched his face. She cleared her throat. "Don't stop. Keep moving."

"That's exactly right. Don't stop. Keep moving." He nodded toward his assistant. "Great job, Ms. Vreeland. Thank you for your help." He led the applause as she made a small bow and returned to her seat.

"Anybody know why I talk about stranger danger at the beginning of every school year?" He raised his hand, indicating how he wanted them to answer.

"Mrs. Peeper makes you."

He laughed. Man, he loved these kids. "Very true. But it's more than that." He pulled a stuffed animal from his props box. "I want you to be wise like my buddy here, the owl. Village Green is a good town, a safe place to grow up, and I don't expect any of you to be approached by a stranger. But I talk about this each year because the owl and I know how important it is to be prepared, to think through how you would react in a dangerous situation, so if one came up, you'd be ready to act wisely."

"If a bad guy came around, you could shoot him."

Sam rested his hand on his holstered gun, always an object of morbid fascination with the kids. He hated bringing a weapon into the school, a tool of violence in a place of learning, yet it was part of his uniform, a fact of life. "I'll do whatever I have to, to keep our citizens safe, but my number one job is to protect people, not to shoot them.

"Okay. That wraps up what I wanted to say." He replaced the owl in the box and turned to Ms. Vreeland. "I had a great time here this morning. Thank you for letting me visit your class."

She stood. "Let's give Officer Sam a round of applause to thank him for talking to us today."

They clapped, and a couple kids popped out of their seats to hug him. Pretty soon everyone was clustered around him, waiting for their turn.

She watched the interaction for several moments, whether pleased or annoyed he couldn't tell, before clearing her throat. "Okay, once everyone has had the opportunity to thank Officer Sam, please go back to your desk and sit."

The noise abated as one by one they returned to their seats.

"I have an idea I'd like to run by Officer Sam."

He paused in the act of scooping up his box, straightening to give her his full attention.

"It's obvious you're a favorite here." She cleared her throat as though she had difficulty getting the words out. "I wonder if it would it be possible for you to come back and visit us?"

Wow, he didn't see that coming. "I'd be happy to."

"If you have time in your schedule, we would love to have you visit . . . once a month. You could bring a favorite book to read to us. Something that would help us to become wise."

"Please! Please!" The kids chimed in with their approval.

Once a month? She was full of surprises. Was it possible he'd read her wrong? That she actually liked having him around? "Okay, sure. I can do that."

"Once you look at your schedule, you can call the school office and set up a time. They'll let me know what you decide."

*In other words, I don't want to talk to you.* That cleared up any lingering questions. For whatever reason, she was willing to have him there, but only just barely.

Not that he'd harbored any illusions about the two of them. She was single and pretty, but clearly had issues—whether just with him or with law enforcement in general he didn't know. Whatever. As much as he enjoyed a good mystery, he didn't need that kind of complication in his personal life.

"Sounds like a plan." He picked up the cardboard box. "See you next month."

# CHAPTER THREE

Riley pulled her SUV into the detached garage, switching off the engine and lowering the garage door simultaneously. She waited until the door was completely down, checking that no one slipped in before climbing out of the vehicle. She never thought she'd be one of those people who shut themselves away from the neighbors, but then she'd never thought she'd be hiding out.

She circled around the front of the car, skirting the row of long-handled rakes and tools hanging neatly on the wall of the garage, to open the passenger door and collect her three plastic bags of groceries, work tote, and purse. The load would be more reasonable if she made two trips, but more trips meant more exposure, and more exposure could lead to discovery.

With a deep breath for courage, she opened the side door of the garage leading into the privacy-fenced backyard and muscled the heavy bags through the opening. Senses on full alert, she swiveled her head from side to side, scanning the area.

All clear.

Bags slapping against her legs, she darted across the short distance to the back entrance, unlocked the door, and ducked inside. Once in the house, she stopped, checking for evidence that anything had been disturbed, listening over the pounding of her heart for any sound of intruders. Satisfied she was alone, she lowered her parcels to the floor with a sigh and relocked the door.

This was ridiculous. She hated the cowardly behavior—the hundreds of cowardly acts she performed each day.

Since she'd been in Texas, things had progressed from bad to worse. Instead of finding freedom in her new location, she'd become a prisoner of her fears.

It had to stop. If she wanted to crawl out of this dark place, she needed to stop looking over her shoulder and silence her increasingly frightening imagination. All she had to do was tell herself the truth.

*It was over.*

Ron had undoubtedly moved on by now. They'd known each other only two months before she pulled her little disappearing act—too short a time to make a lasting attachment. Surely when he realized she wasn't coming back, he'd switch his oppressive attentions to someone else.

She'd met him at her father's funeral. A big man with an athletic build, probably in his late thirties, Ron had introduced himself after the service. He'd said he'd known her parents through classes at the local college and had been so influenced by them that when he'd seen the obituary in the paper, he'd felt compelled to pay his respects. He was sorry to have missed her mother's funeral the year before, but he'd been serving at an overseas mission and was unable to get away. They'd bonded over their mutual admiration for her parents.

Two days later he'd called her—she had no idea how he got her number—and invited her to meet him at the local park for a walk. She'd balked, unwilling to go when her grief was so raw, but he'd gently persuaded her that a little fresh air and exercise would do her good.

He was right. The long stroll in the cool of the morning helped clear some of the tangle in her mind.

Ron was a comfortable companion, the kind of person who always knew just what to say. Better yet, he knew when to be silent. Having lost both of his parents, he was no stranger to grief and offered her a friendly, sympathetic ear.

It had been easy to talk with him about her concerns. When he asked about estate details and she confirmed that the waiting mountain of paperwork weighed heavily on her, he kindly offered to help her in any way he could. He was some kind of financial advisor, helping ministries and individuals navigate the legal ins and outs of managing their money.

She remembered thinking how lucky she was to have met him.

Sometime over the course of the morning, she realized she'd monopolized the conversation and turned the spotlight on him. Ron was less forthcoming about himself, explaining briefly he was the only child of missionary parents, and when they passed away, he'd returned to the States. She chalked up his reluctance to go into detail as lingering grief.

He did share that his lifelong ambition was to be in law enforcement. He told her he'd recently completed the training program at the Oklahoma City Police Academy and made many good friends on the force. He said he was waiting in daily anticipation for the call that a slot had opened up so he could take his place among his uniformed brothers.

She'd laughed at the disparity between a financial advisor and a cop, and he explained that both jobs allowed him to serve people, and joining the police brought the added bonus of gaining the family he missed.

When they returned to their cars an hour later, he asked if she'd meet him for coffee the next day. She accepted the no-pressure invitation because it *had* felt good to get out.

Soon they were seeing each other nearly every day, meeting either for a walk or a cup of coffee. Nothing serious.

She couldn't pinpoint the exact moment when things started to feel "off."

His declaration of undying love for her after two weeks was probably the first red flag. Even with her then-healthy self-confidence, she didn't think she was the sort of person to inspire such reckless devotion. They were barely friends, more exercise buddies who occasionally enjoyed a mocha latte.

In response to his unwelcome and uncomfortable announcement, she decided to pull back. She declined his invitations to walk and offers to meet for coffee.

She was kind but firm. She needed time alone.

He showed up at her house.

Since she hadn't told him where she lived, she'd been shocked when he popped by in the evening with a bunch of flowers to let her know he was thinking of her.

It got creepier. Suddenly, he was everywhere she was. Waiting outside her bank when she'd gone to make a deposit, checking out at the lane next to hers at the grocery store, waiting behind her at the gas station.

It went from surprising coincidence to completely unnerving overnight.

He was stalking her.

Still, she was confident it was all just a misunderstanding. Ron had always been kind and thoughtful. He was a missionary's kid and future law enforcement. As good-looking as he was, he was probably unused to rejection.

She'd just have to be more firm.

Next time he showed up on her doorstep, a pink teddy bear in hand, she invited him in. After placing the stuffed animal on a nearby table, she looked directly into his eyes. "Ron, you're the kindest guy, and I'm so grateful for everything you've done for me, but it has to stop. I don't want you to bring me any more flowers or gifts. I don't want to run into you everywhere I go. I think it's best you don't call or text me. I can see there's no future for us as a couple, and honestly, right now, I don't have it in me to be your friend."

Something threatening came over his handsome face, showed in his eyes. A warning went off in her head, but before she could move, he grabbed her by her upper arms and squeezed so hard it felt as though he would crush her bones.

"No, princess." His brutal tone sounded nothing like his normal voice. "I'm not going anywhere."

Tears of pain and fear filled her eyes.

Just that quickly, he'd wrapped her into a suffocating embrace, apologizing profusely. "I'm so sorry. You know I love you. I'm crazy about you. I wouldn't have hurt you if you hadn't said that." He stroked a large hand down the side of her face, the same hand that left bruises on her arm. "Don't worry. I'm not mad at you. I understand you're not thinking clearly with the grief. You must trust me to know what's best. We're good for each other. A team. You need me."

Nodding, she'd acted as though she'd accepted his apology, but the damage was done. She'd seen the rage in his eyes before he masked it.

The red flag in her mind grew to the size of the flags flown over car dealerships. What had felt *not right* was definitely all wrong.

And she was terrified.

She'd ushered him from the house that night with a false smile and a submissive request for some time to grieve for her father. When she closed and locked the door behind him, she knew she was in trouble. He'd never leave her alone. She had to get out.

Riley scrubbed her hands over her face and returned her thoughts to the present. She unpacked the sacks of groceries, putting the cold items in the refrigerator first. Since moving to Texas, she'd shopped several times at the local grocery, carefully alternating the days to avoid creating a pattern. Ron had been quick to pick up on her habits, forcing *coincidences* to insinuate himself into her life. She was working on becoming less predictable.

*Enough!* She fitted the bottle of milk onto the door and pushed it shut. Ron was in the past. Time to move on, as he undoubtedly had, and embrace her new life.

As she put away the box of cereal and tea bags inside the spacious pantry, she purposefully focused on the moment. She loved her cozy rental house. The owners had updated it without losing any of the charm of the old Craftsman style. Here in the kitchen, they'd painted the cabinets a pretty dove gray and covered the long countertop in gleaming black granite. The nickel hardware was obviously new but in an antique style. Except for the tiled bathrooms, gorgeous dark hardwood floors, certainly original, ran throughout the home.

The Coopers left most everything behind. Their furniture, dishes, pots and pans, even several closets full of clothing awaited their decision to return after Mrs. Cooper's treatments or stay close to their daughter and doctors. The fully furnished home had been a godsend. Sneaking out of her own home in the dead of night, Riley had brought only her clothes and the classroom décor she'd stored in tubs. Here she had everything she needed until she could get back to Oklahoma and sort out her life.

Groceries neatly stashed, Riley carried her work tote to the dining room and unpacked the contents onto the table. A file of papers to be graded, the hard copy of her lesson plans, and a bulging envelope of twenty handmade get-well cards, each crafted of construction paper, glitter, and glue. Tomorrow after school, she'd take them to the post office, bundle them into a mailer, and send them off to Mrs. Cooper.

Too early to start dinner, she settled onto one of the upholstered chairs to look through the stack. She'd just picked up Olivia's card, not surprisingly a work of art, when she heard footfalls on the front porch, followed by a brisk knock.

Her heart shot to her throat, and the card slipped through her suddenly nerveless fingers.

*He'd found her.*

"No. No." She fought for clarity through the wave of panic. "He's moved on. He doesn't know I'm here."

Still, she wasn't expecting anyone. The only person who ever showed up at her door was Mary Jo from down the street, and she never came by without calling first.

A second knock. More insistent.

She levered up from the table, moving on trembling legs. She peeked through the shuttered window to the left of the door. The person knocking was beyond her field of vision, but a familiar police car stood at the curb.

Officer Sam?

The cold burst of fear became a hot rush of fury. She'd specifically told him to set up a reading time with the school office so he wouldn't bother her. She unlocked the door, ready to blast him with the full force of her anger when she noticed the bedraggled bundle in his arms. "Oh!" Pushing open the storm door for him to enter, she asked, "What have you got?"

"Abandoned dog." He wasn't wearing his usual Officer-Cheerful smile. "Found her on the highway just south of town."

Two pitiful dark eyes peered up at Riley. "Poor little thing. Who would do that to an animal?"

"I don't know." He glanced down at the blanket-wrapped creature. "It happens fairly often, but each time I'm surprised."

She heard the sadness in his voice. Interesting. She would have thought law enforcement would have left him jaded. "Why'd you bring her here?"

He looked from the dog cradled in his arms to her and gave a puzzled shrug. "I'm not entirely sure. I guess because she reminded me of you."

"I remind you of a dog?" Hands on hips, she sniffed. "A bad-smelling dog?"

He had the grace to look self-conscious as he laughed. "Sorry. That didn't come out right. Tilting his head, he gave her another considering look. "Although there is a little similarity around the eyes."

She frowned. "My eyes are green."

"The likeness isn't the color. It's the expression. You both look like you've seen some hard times and could use a friend." He side-stepped her and headed toward the hall.

"I ... uh ... hey, where are you going?"

He called over his shoulder. "I thought you'd appreciate it if I gave her a bath."

"I do. That's lovely. But you don't need to do it here, do you?" She wrinkled her nose. "In *my* nice clean tub?"

"Where else would I do it? That way she'll be clean and dry when you feed her."

Riley thought about her newly refilled pantry. Everything but dog food. "What will I feed her?" She trotted after him. "Better question, *why* would I feed her?"

The look he gave her suggested she was a little slow. "People feed their dogs because they can't feed themselves. It's the wrappers. Dogs can't get them open without opposable thumbs."

People feed *their* dogs? Uh oh. He planned to unload the animal on her. "Nuh uh." She shook her head and lifted her palms as if warding off an attack. "No way. That's not *my* dog."

"Why not? You allergic to them?"

"No, of course not. But I don't want one. I'm uh—I'm a teacher."

"Teachers have dogs."

"Not this one." She racked her brain for an excuse when a brilliant thought came to mind. "I can't have a pet." She gestured around them. "This is a rental."

His frown said she'd stumped him. "I thought about that." Then he grinned. "So I called the Coopers on my way over here and explained the situation. They said it was fine."

"You called the Coopers?" She was so angry she sputtered. "You contacted my landlords without asking me first?"

The look on his face said he clearly had no idea what he'd done wrong. "Did I overstep? Sorry. I think I mentioned I go way back with them. First-grade teacher, Boy Scout leader. Never occurred to me you'd mind me talking to them."

"Of course I mind. You went behind my back."

He put up a hand for silence. "Do you like dogs?"

"Well, yes, but—"

"This girl's in a rough place. She's got nowhere to live and nobody to look after her. She's seen some hard times and needs a friend right now. Seems to me you've got the kindness she needs to heal, and I'm pretty sure you could use a friend as well."

"Got any shampoo?" Sam watched Riley closely. Her reaction so far had not been what he had expected.

Then again, what *had* he expected, showing up on her front porch with an abandoned mutt?

Riley huffed out an exasperated breath. "Not for dogs." She may have given in, but not graciously.

"People shampoo is fine."

"The only people shampoo I have costs thirty dollars a bottle."

He shrugged. "That'll work. Our little lady here can pretend she's at some high-end spa."

Riley narrowed her eyes at him before flipping her hair and stomping off toward the back of the house, presumably in search of the overpriced soap.

He lifted the dog higher against his chest to whisper in her ear. "See, I told you not to worry. I can tell she's really going to like you."

He'd spotted the dog along the highway, a mile or so south of town. Midsized, of indeterminate color, she'd been wandering along the side of the road, dangerously close to traffic. He'd driven several yards ahead of her before pulling onto the shoulder. When he got out of the car and called to her, she approached tentatively, crouching low, her scraggly tail wagging frantically. Twice, he'd moved too quickly and spooked her, causing her to retreat to a safe distance. And they would start the process again.

Finally, Sam earned enough trust that she allowed him to lower a collar over her head and lead her back to his vehicle. She waited politely for him to spread the blanket he kept for emergencies over the back seat before hopping in and making herself comfortable. Ordinarily he drove strays directly to the animal shelter in Corsicana, but something about the wounded look in her dark eyes stopped him. Wariness and vulnerability—a look he'd seen recently in another pair of eyes—was a potent combination in dogs *or* women.

His rumbling chuckle caused the dog to shift in his arms.

Judging by the expression on Riley's face earlier, comparing her to a dog had not been his best move. Of course, he'd never been one to dazzle the ladies. Just one more reason why his two best friends had paired off while he sat home on weekends, researching dating sites.

She reappeared in the hall, still miffed, bottle in hand.

"That the liquid gold?" He nodded toward the plastic container.

"Yes, and I hope you don't plan to use all of it." Her nose was clearly out of joint. "It has to be special ordered."

"I'll be very frugal." He glanced around. "Which bathroom do you want me to use?"

Eyes wide in mock surprise, she clapped her hands to her cheeks. "You're asking me? How refreshing. I figured you'd have already commandeered the tub and the best towels."

"Not without your permission. I'd hate to be pushy."

"Ha! Your middle name should be Pushy." She directed him into the hall bathroom, flipped on the light, and followed him inside. "So how exactly does this work?"

He glanced at her in surprise. "You've never washed a dog?"

She shook her head. "I've never had a pet."

He frowned. "That's tragic. Every kid ought to have a dog."

"Did you?"

"Sure. We always had at least one." He shifted his canine bundle to one side and turned on the tub faucet, holding his hand under the flow to monitor the temperature of the water.

Riley stood behind his left shoulder. "If you're such an animal lover, why don't you keep her?"

Once the water reached a comfortable temperature, he lowered the stopper in the drain. "Can't. I've got a cat."

"I wouldn't have taken you for a cat person." Her skepticism rang out loud and clear.

He shrugged. "I pretty much like all animals. I inherited Princess when a neighbor of mine went into a nursing home and nobody wanted to take her cat."

"Princess?" Riley snickered. "You have a cat named Princess? Remind me not to ask for your help finding dog names."

"Deal." He hid his smile at the mention of naming the dog. Sounded like she was at least entertaining the idea of pet ownership.

After kneeling on the rug beside the tub, he gently unwrapped the dog from the towel. She remained calm, her big brown eyes trusting, as he lowered her into the warm, shallow water.

Riley inched closer. "Omigosh! Look at the filth running off her." She fanned her face and took a step back. "And the smell."

Sam focused on breathing through his mouth. "Can you find us a glass or pitcher to use for rinsing?"

She hurried from the bathroom, returning seconds later with a tall plastic pitcher in one hand. Her other hand was over her nose. "This work?"

"Perfect." He steadied the dog while he slowly poured water over her, dirt and whatever sluicing into the tub and down the drain. He emptied the water twice before he could get around to soaping her.

"She acts like she likes it." Riley knelt beside him, watching as he lathered the dog.

He nodded as he worked. "She'll feel and smell a whole lot better. Of course, the shampoo won't take care of the fleas."

Riley squeaked and sprang to her feet. "You brought me a dog with fleas?"

*Probably could have finessed that into the conversation a little better.* "I haven't seen any yet, but yeah, it's a real possibility. Keep her outside tonight. She'll be fine on a pallet by the back door. I'll pick up some flea soap for her tomorrow."

"Never mind. I'll get it." After a thoughtful pause she asked, "Does anyone around here sell flea soap?"

"Buchanan's Hardware. He carries all kinds of pet supplies and food." After a final rinse, he shut off the water. "Grab me a couple towels, will you?"

Riley stepped over his legs to open the door of the cabinet beside the tub. She pulled out two pink ones and handed them to him. "I got these from the bottom of the stack. I hope they're not Mrs. Cooper's favorites."

"No worries. I'll take them home and wash them in really hot water a couple times and they'll be as good as new." He lifted the dog onto one of the towels, ruffling her wet fur with the other.

Riley watched the process from a safe distance. "Poor baby. She's nothing but skin and bones."

He'd thought the same thing as he'd washed her and could count every rib. "It's okay. You'll have her fattened up in no time."

"Is the hardware store open now? If you tell me where it is, I'll go pick up some food."

He shook his head. "They close at six. No problem. She can eat whatever you're having for dinner."

"Dogs eat Fruit Loops?" She grinned at his horrified expression, clearly delighted at having pulled one over on him. "Ha! Just kidding. I've got some chicken. Think she'll eat that?"

"As long as you pick out the bones, she'll love it."

"Let me get it started." She gingerly patted the dog's head and walked out.

"What'd I tell you?" he whispered to the dog. "You two are already well on your way to being BFFs."

He pulled the towel away, and she shook herself, sending water droplets flying everywhere. "Hey, that's no way to endear yourself around here. Remember, we're trying to convince her to let you stay." He used a dry corner of the towel to mop up the spray.

The motion fluffed her mid-length fur, adding a little soft volume to her pitiful frame. Sitting on his heels, he stroked a hand across her back. Now that she was clean, he could tell she was mostly black with a white bib and three white paws. "Look at you. What a pretty girl you are. And you smell better too. A couple weeks of steady meals, and you'll be good as new."

The dog licked his hand as he scratched behind her now-soft ear. "You're welcome. I'm happy to help. To be honest, I wasn't being entirely unselfish by bringing you here."

"Are you talking to the dog?" Riley called from the kitchen.

"No way. That's weird." He leaned closer to whisper, "You should know this rescue thing goes both ways. Your new owner needs you at least as much as you need her. Just don't tell her I said so."

Riley appeared in the doorway. "You *are* talking to the dog."

"Do you mind?" With a feigned look of indignation, he turned his back on her. "This is a *private* conversation."

She laughed as he'd intended. "I brought you a plastic trash bag for the blanket and towels."

"Thanks." He placed it on the counter behind him. "I'll return the towels when they're clean."

"No, just bring them by the school when you come to read to the class."

Another pointed reminder in case he'd forgotten the other half dozen she'd sent his way, that she wasn't interested in anything beyond a professional connection. He gave a mental shrug. He could live with that. "I was surprised you invited me to come back to your class."

"I surprised myself." She gave a self-conscious laugh. "I had just finished praying God would show me if there was anything I could do to bring balance to my kids' lives when you came in to do your safety spiel. After seeing how well you interacted with them, I figured you might be my answer. Lots of my students are living in one-parent homes, usually with the mother, and I don't want them to miss out on having the benefit of a strong female *and* male influence in their lives."

The opening was too good to pass up. "So, what you're saying is I'm the answer to your prayers."

She snorted and rolled her eyes. "Puhlease."

"Don't worry." He struck a pose. "I'm not the kind to let it go to my head."

Riley laughed. "Good. As a side benefit, I think it will help the kids see that police are real people. They like children, read books, and talk to dogs."

"I'm sure I speak for law enforcement everywhere when I say thank you for the positive press." The dog remained seated on the rug as he levered up off his knees to face Riley. "I wouldn't have taken you for an advocate. The first time I met you, I got the impression you couldn't be rid of me quick enough."

She lifted her shoulders in a dismissive shrug. "Maybe I don't like big sweaty men."

"Makes sense, except I wasn't sweating when I first arrived. You took one look at the uniform and car, and nearly passed out."

"It was the heat." At his look of disbelief, she added, "And you surprised me, that's all. I wasn't expecting to see a cop."

Folding his arms across his chest, he leaned against the counter and cocked a brow, inviting a confession. "You have a bad experience with the police in Oklahoma?"

There it was again, that flicker of fear in her eyes. She quickly dropped her gaze. "No, I can't say that I have. I don't know any personally. I did get a speeding ticket once, but I totally deserved it, so no hard feelings there."

"Good. Because I wouldn't want you to judge all of us based on one bad one."

"Haven't you been telling me you are the good guys?"

"We are. And we work really hard to screen our people. But occasionally a bad one slips through." *And invariably makes headlines.* He shrugged. "I hate it, but it happens."

She gave him a searching look. "And do the bad ones have the same loyalty of the force?"

He frowned. "I'm not sure what you're asking."

She developed a sudden interest in the doorframe, watching as she traced a hand along the painted wood. "A person once described the police to me as a brotherhood. Like a fraternity. Each one has the back of the others."

"That's true."

"So, what if a bad one wanted to use police resources for personal reasons?" She lifted her eyes to his. "Would the brotherhood back him up?"

The hypothetical question was strangely specific. "Like helping him carry out a vendetta?" He shook his head. "No. There are procedures and safeguards built into the system to prevent misuse of resources. I suppose they could try, but by sticking their neck out for this bad one, they would jeopardize their own career. Nobody wants to do that."

Eyes on his face, she nodded slowly, as if digesting what he'd said. Instead of saying more and giving him a clue as to what she was thinking, she changed the subject. "I bet the chicken is almost ready."

"Great. She can eat her dinner while I clean out the tub."

"I'm glad you offered because no way I'm touching that." She gestured toward the less-than-pristine tub. "There's a sponge and cleanser under the sink. You can join us in the kitchen when you're done."

He opened his mouth to explain it would take a while before the dog was comfortable enough with her to follow her, when the dog hopped up and trotted out behind Riley as if she'd been doing it all her life. He rolled his eyes heavenward. "Women."

Careful so as not to splash the bleach solution on his uniform, he scrubbed and rinsed the tub twice before he was satisfied. Once finished, he tucked the dirty blanket and towels into the trash bag and walked out to the kitchen.

The dog stood at Riley's feet, eating dainty bites of chicken off one of Mrs. Cooper's china plates.

Riley frowned up at him. "I've given her most of a chicken breast, and she still seems hungry. Do I keep feeding her until she stops?"

"I wouldn't. Stick with several small meals for a day or two to give her stomach time to adapt to real food." He glanced around. "Okay, looks like you two have got it, so I'm out of here."

"Wait!" Riley reached out a hand to stop him. "You're not leaving, are you?"

"Yeah. I'm actually on duty."

"You can't go." Her voice climbed an octave. "I don't know anything about dogs. What do I use for her bed?"

"Now that she's eaten, put her in the backyard. She should stay outside until you've dealt with the fleas. You can use the rug from the bathroom for her bed. It's soft and washable. Just lay it outside by the door. Put her on it once, so she knows it's hers, and she should be good to go."

"Easy peasy." Riley's doubtful expression said it was anything but.

"If you have a problem, give me a call."

"I don't have your number."

"Sure you do. I gave it—" He caught the guilty look on her face and laughed. "You threw it away. No matter." Backtracking to the desk, he picked up a sticky note off the pad, rewrote his information and placed it in her outstretched hand. "Try to hold onto this. It may come in handy."

Bending, he gave the dog a last scratch. "You girls take care of each other."

"I guess I should be thanking you for bringing her by."

Delighted she'd come to recognize the blessing he'd bestowed on her, he lowered his head modestly to receive her gratitude. "Not necessary."

"Good, because I'm still not sure I'm thankful."

He was laughing as she walked him through the dining room. He paused, pointing to the artwork spread out on the surface of the table. "What's all this?"

"They're get-well cards. My class made them for Mrs. Cooper."

Picking one up by the corner, he studied the interesting combination of glitter and globs of dried glue. "They're really great."

"The kids ask about her all the time. I thought it would be nice to make her something, so she'd know people here were thinking of her." She pressed her lips together. "You don't think it's presumptuous, do you? I don't actually know her . . ."

"It's a very thoughtful gesture." He replaced the card on the stack and gave her a reassuring smile. "She'll love it. I promise."

"Good." She escorted him to the door, waiting as he stepped out onto the porch and headed down the stairs, the plastic bag swinging against his calves.

Almost to his car, he had a thought and turned toward her. "Hey, when you're at the hardware store picking up food and flea soap, ask if they have anything for worms."

"Worms?" He heard a touch of high-pitched hysteria in her voice. "Did you say worms?"

He nodded and waved before ducking into the squad car. He could hear her screeching as he pulled away from the curb.

*Talk about finesse.* Who said he didn't have a way with the ladies?

# CHAPTER FOUR

Riley got up an hour early to cut fruit for her class. Unlike the grocery stores back home that offered convenient tubs of precut, fresh produce, the Grocery Giant in Village Green carried its fresh items in their unwashed, unpeeled, and uncut form. Since it was always fresh and usually locally sourced, she had no real complaint.

She washed and hulled a quart of strawberries, halving them before tossing them on top of the grapes and melon cubes in the green plastic bowl. Satisfied she had enough to feed twenty growing bodies, she snapped on the lid and placed the bowl on the kitchen table next to her purse and work tote.

Shadow hovered at her feet.

"I'm leaving early today," Riley explained to her ever-present companion. "But I'll be back as soon as school's out. No errands to run."

The dog wagged her tail as though she understood and approved her plan.

"Today's Friday, so we'll have the whole weekend together."

The wagging intensified, setting Shadow's entire body into joyful motion. Riley bent to rub her behind the ears. "You're such a good girl."

Two weeks ago, she'd had no idea having a pet could be such a blessing. Once they'd got past the fleas and internal parasites—she shuddered at the too-recent memory—things had been smooth sailing. The man at the hardware store helped her find the right food and flea products and set the dog up for shots when the Corsicana Shelter was in town for their monthly pet clinic.

Once her pest problems were behind them—another shudder—Shadow moved seamlessly into her life. Beyond being good company, she proved to be an attentive watchdog, barking the alert when someone was on the property, and a courteous roommate who thoughtfully restricted her *business* to the outside.

Both Saturday nights they'd snuggled side by side on the sofa, on a blanket to protect Mrs. Cooper's upholstery, and watched romantic comedies. They shared a bowl of popcorn with extra butter—the man at the hardware store assured her it was okay for an occasional treat.

Though the fancy monogrammed dog bed Riley ordered off the internet finally arrived, Shadow preferred to curl up on the floor beside Riley's bed at night, always within arm's reach. Once her owner was tucked in and the lights out, she'd turn two circles, then settle in with a loud sigh.

Riley slept better since Shadow arrived, frequently resting so soundly she'd go the whole night without waking up, a luxury she hadn't enjoyed since leaving Oklahoma. The times she wasn't so peaceful, or a sound awakened her, she had her faithful friend beside her to help investigate.

"I guess I'd better get going." Riley walked to the front window as she did every morning, peeking through the blinds to be certain no one awaited her outside. "Coast is clear."

The dog's soft chocolate brown eyes gave her a look of compassionate understanding, as though she knew the daily ritual was paranoid but wasn't passing judgment. They walked back to the kitchen. Riley gave her one last scratch before gathering her belongings and the bowl of fruit in one hand, her keys in the other.

"Have a great day. I'll see you after school."

After pushing aside the short, ruffled curtains on the window of the back door to check for intruders, Riley stepped into the backyard, quickly locked up behind her, and hurried to the garage.

In her ongoing effort to put the past behind her, every morning as she backed out of the driveway, she made a point to remind herself Ron had forgotten her by now. The nightmare was over. He was history.

Some days she almost believed it.

However, she continued the surveillance and erratic schedule. Just in case.

There were only a few cars in the school parking lot, all familiar, when she pulled in a little before seven. With her key badge ready in one hand, her bags on her arm, and the bowl clutched to her chest, she darted up the wide concrete sidewalk, swiped her ID, and slipped into the building. The door swung closed with a sigh and relocked with a reassuring click.

Once inside the safety of the building, she slowed to a more decorous pace. Her footfalls rang out on the tile floor of the empty corridor as she passed the glass-front administrative office, turned right into the first hall, and down to the fourth room on the right. Dropping her key badge into her bag, she freed a hand to straighten the orange plaid bow on the fall wreath she'd hung on the classroom door.

"Good morning." Mrs. Peeper simultaneously rapped the door frame and stepped into the room several paces behind Riley. She must have noticed Riley's nervous jump. "Oops. Sorry, did I scare you?"

Riley nodded, clapping a hand over her racing heart. "Good morning. You're here early."

"Habit. I saw you come in and I thought I'd take a minute to touch base with you." The principal stopped in the center of the room, turning a slow circle. "I love what you've done in here. You may not know it, but you've got the teacher's lounge buzzing about your creativity."

"Thank you." Riley set her things on the desk before letting her gaze sweep the colorful room she'd spent hours decorating. "I think it's a combination of internet overload and too much time on my hands."

"You don't give yourself enough credit. You're obviously very talented." Mrs. Peeper moved closer, her intelligent eyes locking on Riley's. "I came by to ask you how it's going? It's been a month now. Do you feel your transition to the school has gone well? Are you enjoying your job?"

In Riley's opinion, Mrs. Peeper was the perfect principal. A high-energy woman in her early sixties with a chic, short hairstyle and a penchant for tailored suits, she was deeply involved with the students and staff without crossing the invisible line into interference and micromanagement.

"I love the job. The kids are fantastic, and the staff is so kind and supportive. It's a great school."

Her boss accepted the praise with a modest nod. "Thank you. I'm proud of it. I've got a super team. Every one of you is worth your weight in gold." Her gaze came to rest on the plastic bowl sitting on the desk. "Wow, big lunch!"

Riley laughed. "It's a fruit salad for the kids. We've been doing a unit on food and nutrition, and I thought it would be a good hands-on way to reinforce the concepts." She placed her hand on the lid. "And honestly, I'm trying to sneak extra food into some of the kids—well, one in particular—without being obvious."

The principal looked up sharply. "Which one?"

"Chris Enslow. I've noticed his lunch has been really sparse this last week or so. Half a peanut butter sandwich or a small tub of dry cereal. Not enough for a growing boy."

The older woman pursed her lips. "Hmm, his mother is very conscientious. I wonder if there's a problem?"

"I haven't asked. I'm waiting for him to tell me." Riley grinned. "First graders are so open. If you give them enough time, they'll tell you everything about their lives."

Mrs. Peeper chuckled. "It's a sweet age." She grew thoughtful. "Officer Sam is coming by to read to your class today, isn't he? Why don't you send him to me when he's finished? I'll ask him to make a check on the Enslows. Just to be sure everything is okay."

Riley caught the corner of her lip in her teeth. "I would hate for them to think I sicced the police on them."

The principal waved away her concern. "I never worry about Sam. He's very discreet."

She propped a hip on the corner of Riley's desk and folded her arms across her chest. "I really like your idea of having him read to the kids once a month. He's agreed to read to the other class of first graders too. I mentioned the arrangement at a conference I attended last week, and several district principals said they were going to implement something similar in their own schools."

As she stowed her bag in the bottom desk drawer, Riley thought about how well Sam interacted with the kids. "They'll have a hard time finding someone like Sam."

"He's special, isn't he?"

Uh-oh. Something in Mrs. Peeper's tone made it sound like she thought Riley had a *thing* for him. She straightened and looked her in the eye. "I only meant they need to find someone who works really well with kids. Sam's very bighearted."

Her boss gave her a knowing nod, as though she didn't believe a word she'd said, before heading toward the door. Something on the bulletin board caused her to stop. She pointed to a small photograph tacked in the corner. "Is that Mrs. Cooper?"

"Yes." Riley joined her in front of the display. "She sent us that picture with her last letter."

The principal beamed. "Elizabeth Cooper is an incredible woman and a dear friend. She called me when she got the big box of cards your class made. She said it was the nicest gift she'd ever received."

With a sigh of part pleasure, part relief, Riley laid a hand over her heart. "I'm so glad. The kids had fun making them. They were over the moon when she wrote back and asked us to be her pen pals. We've already sent off our first batch of response letters. It's excellent practice for their writing skills."

"And an immeasurable blessing for a sick woman." Mrs. Peeper stepped into the hallway and turned back to face her with a glowing smile. "I don't think Officer Sam is the only one around here with a big heart. I'm very glad you're on our team, Riley." With a wave, she left.

As arranged, Officer Sam arrived after recess. He knocked on the open door as he ducked his head in. "Hi, Ms. Vreeland. Is this a good time for a story?"

The class broke out into enthusiastic whoops, and Riley set aside the papers she had been grading to greet him. If he noticed the tangy smell of twenty sweaty little bodies just in from the heat of late September, he was too much the gentleman to say so.

"It's perfect." She smiled, surprised to discover she was genuinely pleased to see him. It wasn't that they were friends or that she'd missed him, but the man who brought her Shadow would always have a place in her heart. She directed him to the adult-sized chair she'd placed in the front center of the room. "Why don't you sit here where everyone can see and hear you?"

"This is great." A dimple showed in his right cheek as he settled in. "Thanks."

She nodded toward the book in his hands. "What did you bring to read to us today?"

He held it up, first to her, then slowly panning the room to show the class. "It's called *Cross My Heart,* by C. LeBlanc." His gaze rested meaningfully on hers. "It's about trust."

Ignoring the look and any message he was trying to communicate, she turned to the students. "Sounds great. I'll have a seat and you can get started."

She sat at her desk, angling her body so she faced him, and nodded for him to begin.

Officer Sam was a natural. He infused just enough inflection into his rich baritone to give life to the animal characters without sounding patronizing or childish. He held the book open at his shoulder, careful to display the pictures as he read, then another time before he turned the page.

*She could fall for a guy who related so well to children.*

The thought caught her by surprise. She wasn't looking for a man, especially not after she'd worked so diligently to shake one loose. And when she *did* decide she was ready to date, it wouldn't be a cop. No, thank you. She preferred a scholar to a superhero.

Only . . . Sam didn't look much like a warrior just now. Sitting tall in his chair, his knees wide and torso slightly forward, he was caught up in the story and his young audience.

For a second, she allowed herself to forget the uniform and just enjoy the moment.

"The end." He shut the book with a snap.

The kids gave him an enthusiastic round of applause. Riley stood, clapping as she crossed to him. "Thank you so much. We enjoyed listening to the story."

He nodded his acknowledgment, first to the class, then to her. "I had a great time. Thank you for inviting me."

She lifted her arm to get the attention of the kids. "I want everyone to take out their crayons and a sheet of paper and draw a picture of your favorite part of the book we just heard. You need to do your best, quiet work while I speak to Officer Sam for a moment."

She tilted her head toward the door, indicating he was to step into the hall, and followed him out. "Thank you." She kept her voice just above a whisper. "That was great."

His eyes locked on hers. "Did *you* like the book?"

"It was a good choice. The illustrations were colorful, and it had a great universal message—" She finally acknowledged the pointed look he was giving her, a repetition of the one he'd given her earlier. "What? I don't have a problem with trust."

His mouth quirked up. "If you say so."

She narrowed her eyes. "If you start with the good guy thing again, I won't be responsible for my actions."

"No, ma'am." His brown eyes danced as he shook his head. "It never crossed my mind."

Somehow their conversation had veered into semiflirtatious territory. *Not where she wanted to go.* "Mrs. Peeper wanted me to tell you to stop by her office."

"Okay, sure." His gaze roamed her face. "You look better."

"Meaning I looked bad before?"

He gave a self-conscious chuckle. "That didn't come out right, did it? What I mean is you look . . . well rested."

Hard to fault a man for being honest. "Thank you."

"You and the dog working out?"

Smiling, she nodded. "She's great. Woman's best friend."

He dimpled. "I'm glad. What'd you name her?"

"Shadow."

His attempt at stifling a snort didn't work. "Original."

She grinned. "I guess I deserve that for the jab about a cat named Princess. I admit, naming pets is harder than it looks."

"Must be." Silence stretched between them as he lingered just outside her door. Finally, he straightened and took a step back. "I guess I'll go. See you next month."

Man, he did it again.

He'd never been smooth, but Riley Vreeland brought out a horrifying new level of adolescent awkwardness in him. One small victory. At least he hadn't told her she smelled nice, or that the shampoo smelled as nice on her as it did on the dog.

He waited until she reentered her classroom before heading toward the principal's office. Though he'd never attended County Elementary in its current location, the sights and smells were those of his school memories. Gray-tiled floors imbedded with flecks of color to camouflage the wear, rows of skinny metal lockers lining the halls, and the smell of grease and food mingled with the scent of heated bodies warmed by the recess sun. The sounds of learning drifted through open classroom doors.

He stepped into the front office. "Good afternoon, Ms. Schmidt. Is your boss around?"

The school secretary looked up from her computer screen, squinting through her red cat-eyed glasses. "Hi, Sam. Go right in. She's expecting you."

"Thanks." He walked the short, carpeted hall to the principal's office, knocked twice for courtesy, and entered, pulling the door closed behind him. "Hey, Ms. Peeper. Riley told me you wanted to see me."

Mrs. Peeper smiled and pushed aside the stack of papers she was working on. "Hi, Sam. Have a seat."

He lowered himself into the upholstered armchair across the desk from her, forearms resting on his thighs.

True to form, she didn't waste time on small talk. "Riley mentioned that Chris Enslow's lunch has been especially sparse for the last week or so. It may be nothing—his mother could have missed her regular trip to the grocery store, but Riley was concerned. Do you have time to run by there to ensure everything is okay?"

"I'd be happy to." The beauty of a small town was that it didn't take a dozen or so agencies and a ream of paperwork to look in on a neighbor. Village Green took care of their own.

"Thank you." She gave him a speaking look. "And you'll let me know if there's anything I can do?"

Experience told him those weren't empty words. More than once he'd seen her get involved physically and financially when there was a need in her student body.

"Sure thing." He paused before voicing the question that had been playing in his mind. "So, what do you know about her?"

She frowned. "Chris's mother?"

Shaking his head, he laughed. "Riley Vreeland."

Expression neutral, she lifted a brow. "Beyond the fact she's smart, committed to her students, and very lovely?"

He resisted the temptation to roll his eyes. "I've got that part. How did she get here?"

"By car, I would imagine." Her frown said she didn't like his line of questioning. Riley was clearly a favorite. "Is there a problem?"

He shook his head. "Just curious. I keep asking myself why does a lovely, smart, committed woman—your words—from Oklahoma City choose to bury herself in a place like Village Green?"

Head lowered, she studied her clasped hands for a moment before looking up. "I think she needed a change. She'd just lost both her parents in a relatively short period of time and wanted to get away from the sadness."

*Made sense. But still . . . There was getting away and then there was Village Green.* "She said she found us after reading a travel article and saw the job posting when she researched the city website."

Mrs. Peeper nodded. "She contacted me by email. Apparently, she had a lot of estate matters to handle. She's an only child and requested we conduct her interviews by video conference so she wouldn't have to travel at a critical time. Her credentials impressed me enough that I agreed."

She picked up a pen, rolled it between her hands. "Because I couldn't meet her face-to-face, I did an extra thorough background check on her. I personally called her references and everyone she's ever worked for. They all sing her praises, and I can see why. Ms. Vreeland is a gem."

Maybe so. But until he had all the facts, he was reserving judgment. "The kids seem to like her."

"She's a very likeable young lady." Her sharp eyes zeroed in on his. "And single."

He leaned back in the chair. "Are you adding matchmaker to your job description?"

"Only for special people."

"Would that be me or her?"

Mrs. Peeper grinned. "Both. I've known you all your life, so I'm very familiar with what a terrific young man you are. Though she's a relatively new acquaintance, I can tell she's a wonderful person."

"Thank you for the compliment."

She gave an easy shrug. "It's true. And now that two of the three musketeers have paired off, I think it must be your turn." She put down the pen to give him a penetrating look. "You're not getting any younger, you know."

"Ouch." Painful topic. He and Trey and Joe had been best friends since boyhood. The three musketeers. Recently, both Trey and Joe found the love of their lives. And while he was genuinely happy for them, it stung a little to be the one left behind.

"Think it over." She shifted the stack of paper she'd pushed aside to the center of her desk, a clear sign of dismissal. "Keep me posted on the Enslows. And close the door on your way out."

A little before five, Sam pulled up in front of the Enslow place, a small, white wood frame home on a postage-stamp-sized lot. Even with a full-time job and a child to raise on her own, Darcie always kept the house and yard immaculate. This afternoon her car was in the driveway, and Chris's bike was propped against the concrete stairs of the house across the street.

He bounded up the front steps and rapped on the frame of the screen door.

Darcie appeared, concern written on her face. "Hey, Sam." She pushed open the door and stepped aside for him to enter. "Everything okay?"

The temperature in the house was as uncomfortably warm as the outside. "Sure." He flashed an innocent grin. "Can't an old friend just stop by for a visit?"

Her expression turned wry. "They can, but they usually don't. Especially not in uniform."

He hiked up his shoulders. "End of shift. I was in Chris's class today, and it reminded me I hadn't talked with you in a while."

"He said you came in to read to them. That's really nice." She motioned for him to follow her.

"That's me. Mr. Nice." They walked into the kitchen where a big pot of water boiled on the stove, pumping heat into the already-warm room.

She opened a can of tomato sauce and poured it into a saucepan. "We're having spaghetti for dinner. It'll be ready in thirty minutes if you can stay."

He shook his head. "Sorry, not tonight. I've still got to go back to the station and file my final reports. I'll take a rain check if you're offering."

"Anytime. You're missing a real treat tonight. Chris's teacher brought a big bowl of fruit in for the kids since they're studying nutrition. Apparently, she got carried away while she was cutting and ended up with enough fruit for an army. She asked if I'd be willing to take it off her hands." Darcie's face lit with delight over her good fortune. "I was like . . . are you kidding?"

Apparently the lovely, smart, committed teacher was also generous. The evidence continued to stack up in her favor.

"That's great." With the privilege of an old friend, he pulled out a chair from the table, turned it around, and straddled it. "You've got the windows open. Problem with the air conditioner?"

"No." She shook her head. "I'm just not running it." She stirred the pan before slipping into the seat across from his and lowering her voice. "I lost my job at Burger Barn two weeks ago, so I'm trying to keep the bills down."

"Oh man, I'm sorry."

A woman accustomed to life's hard knocks, she shrugged. "It happens. Honestly, it's for the best. My boss was a jerk, hitting on me all the time. The good news is I got a call today from Simone's. I applied for a job, and they hired me as a waitress. The pay should be better since I'll get tips, and they gave me the breakfast and lunch shift so I can be off in time to pick up Chris from school."

"What time do you have to be there to work breakfast?" Simone's was in Corsicana, a thirty-minute drive.

Darcie grimaced. "Super early. Beth Shaver across the street said I could leave Chris with them in the morning, since they're up early, and she'll take him to school with her kids."

"That works." Perspiration beaded on his forehead, and he pulled the collar away from his neck. "Look Darcie, I'd like to help until you get back on your feet."

She frowned. "No. You've helped enough." A smile broke through. "Chris wouldn't have had a Christmas if it wasn't for Santa Sam. He loves that bike so much, he brings it in at night to keep it out of the weather."

"I'm glad he likes it." A drop of sweat rolled down his back. "You're going to have to get some air conditioning on in here or the bike's gonna melt. Tell you what, why don't you let me cover your electric bill."

Chin up, her pretty face took on a militant expression. "I don't take charity."

He screwed up his mouth. "What charity? Come on, Darcie. We've been friends for what—ten, fifteen years? Friends help each other out in a pinch, right?"

"Yeah, but—"

He lifted a hand to stop her. "No buts. You're a good person going through a bad stretch. Let me help you till you get to the other side."

"Things *are* really tight . . ." She frowned as she weighed his offer. At last, she blew out a breath and nodded hesitantly. "Okay, just this once." She lifted earnest eyes to his. "And I'll pay you back."

"Got the bill handy?"

Standing, she walked to the counter, picked up an envelope from a short stack of mail and placed it in his outstretched hand. "Thank you, Sam."

She detoured to the stove to give the pan another stir. "I've been thinking about getting a roommate to help with expenses. I've got three bedrooms here, seems wrong to let one go to waste when I could use the rent money."

"It might work. But you need to be real smart about who you bring in. I'll be happy to help you interview any applicants before you make a decision."

The front door slammed, and Darcie shot him a warning glance as Chris trotted into the kitchen, a wide grin on his face. "Hi, Officer Sam. I saw your car outside. Are you eating dinner with us?"

Sam folded the bill and slipped it into his shirt pocket. "I wish I was. I've still got work to do tonight. But I'll be back. Maybe we can do a cookout."

Chris beamed. "Hamburgers and hot dogs like last time?"

He nodded. "Hamburgers and hot dogs. I'd better move on." He stood and ruffled a hand through the boy's dark hair. "You take care of your mom, okay?"

"Yes, sir."

Darcie followed him to the front door. He withdrew his wallet from his pocket, pulled out several bills and extended them to her.

She looked at the money, then back up at him. "What's that for?"

Reaching for her hand, he pressed the cash into her palm. "It costs money to feed growing boys."

Raising up on tiptoes, she kissed his cheek. "Thank you, Sam,"

"Are you kidding? That's what friends are for. And Darcie, for heaven's sake, turn on the air."

# CHAPTER FIVE

Riley laid her napkin on the table beside her plate. "Mary Jo, that was wonderful. I ate entirely too much."

The older woman smiled. "You can't quit now. The best is yet to come." She motioned toward the white bakery box on the counter. "I've got two pieces of pumpkin turtle cheesecake from Paradise Bakery for our dessert."

"You had me at pumpkin." Riley placed a hand on her protesting stomach. "I don't know where I'll put it, but I'm not one to back down from a challenge. Especially not where Paradise Bakery is concerned. Eden is a genius."

Mary Jo nodded with obvious pride. "She's got a gift, that's for sure. Have you tried her chocolate mousse torte?"

"Not yet, but it sounds amazing."

"Like a slice of heaven. We'll have some next time you come for dinner."

"Deal." Riley stood and began gathering plates from the table. "I'll take dish detail if you want to serve up dessert."

In the six weeks since Riley moved to Village Green, she'd had dinner with her elderly neighbor half a dozen times. She'd accepted the first invitation only because she couldn't think of a polite way to refuse her, but since then she jumped at the chance to hang out with her. Mary Jo was part gal pal, part substitute mom, and all fun. Wise and loving, as well as a great listener, she helped fill the huge hole left by the death of Riley's parents.

Mary Jo walked her to the door a little past nine. "I swear I gained at least a pound tonight."

Riley paused just inside the threshold. "Everything was delicious." She patted her stomach. "If I had any willpower, I'd go home and do fifty crunches."

Mary Jo sighed. "I keep telling myself I need to get out and walk more."

"Me too. I've noticed Shadow has packed on a few pounds too." An idea occurred to her. "Why don't the three of us go for a walk tomorrow morning, before it gets hot?"

The older woman nodded enthusiastically. "Sounds good. What time?"

Hmm. She didn't want to make it too early as Saturday was her one day to sleep in. "Does eight work for you?"

"Perfect. We can come back here afterwards for coffee and muffins."

Riley laughed. "I think that might defeat the purpose of the walk." She hugged Mary Jo. "Thank you for a lovely evening. I'll see you in the morning."

At the bottom of the porch steps, Riley made a quick scan of the street before hurrying to her SUV. Mary Jo stood waving at the end of the porch. If she thought it was peculiar for a healthy young woman to drive the short block between their houses, she was too kind a friend to say so.

She gave Mary Jo a final wave and ducked into the vehicle, locking the doors. The quiet, well-lit street was empty. She made the block, raised the garage door, and pulled in, lowering it behind her.

"Hey, Shadow, I'm home."

She set her purse on the wooden stool inside the back door and toed off her shoes. "Mary Jo sent you a doggie bag." She jiggled it.

Silence.

A fearsome rush of adrenaline surged through her. Something was wrong. Since the first night Sam brought the dog, Shadow never failed to greet her when she came in.

Riley's heart hammered as she studied the kitchen. Everything was in place, just as she left it. Including the full bowl of food she'd put out for the dog just before she left for school this morning.

"Shadow?" She moved soundlessly along the wood floors through the kitchen, into the dining room and down the hall to her darkened bedroom.

The dog lay on her monogrammed bed in the corner. At the sight of Riley, she lifted her head slightly and thumped her tail.

"Hey girl, what's up? You scared me when you didn't come to the door." Riley crouched to pet her. "Are you shivering? What's the matter, honey? Don't you feel well?"

She stroked the length of the dog's side. Shadow lifted her gaze to Riley's and gave her a pained look before dropping her head against the cushioned bed.

Even a pet novice like herself could see something was terribly wrong. She pushed back a wave of panic. What should she do? Nice Mr. Buchanan at the hardware store, her link to all things canine, was gone for the night, and the only veterinary services they'd ever used were the ones they received from the visiting pet shelter.

She couldn't ignore the look of misery in Shadow's eyes. She had to do something.

Sam.

She could call him. He knew all about dogs, right? Hadn't he said he'd been raised with them his whole life? After a moment of indecision, she stood. "Wait right there. I'll call Sam. He'll know what to do."

She ran to the kitchen desk, shoving aside papers and bills. He'd given her his number. It had to be here somewhere.

At last, she found it. The orange sticky note had attached itself to the back of the house papers the Coopers had left. Her fingers trembled as she entered his number and waited.

"This is Sam."

Just hearing his voice lowered her heart-pounding anxiety several notches. "Sam, it's Riley Vreeland." In case he didn't recognize her name, she added, "From the elementary school."

His chuckle said he hadn't needed the clarification. "Yeah, Riley, what's going on?"

Belatedly, she remembered it was Friday night. "I'm really sorry to bother you, but something's the matter with Shadow. I think she's sick."

"What makes you say so?" The humor was gone from his voice.

Riley's glance fell on the full bowl of dog food. "She hasn't eaten all day. I was out this evening, and when I got home, she didn't greet me at the door. I found her lying on her bed, shivering." Tears filled her eyes and her voice quavered. "Something's wrong, Sam. I'm not sure she can stand."

"I'll be there in five."

Relief washed over her. Help was on the way. "Okay, that's good. Thanks."

She disconnected the call and hurried back to Shadow. "It's going to be all right. Sam's coming."

Less than five minutes later she heard his knock. Even in an emergency, Riley paused to check the side window before opening the door. He stood in a pool of light on the porch, far enough away that she could see him clearly through the glass.

He looked different tonight. No uniform. Off-duty Sam looked good in a snug, gray T-shirt and worn jeans. Really good.

She undid the lock and pushed open the storm door for him to enter. Suddenly self-conscious around the handsome stranger, she ducked her head. "Thank you for coming so quickly. I didn't know what to do, and I panicked."

"Glad to help." The familiar aw-shucks grin helped her regain her footing. He looked different, but he was still Sam.

"She's in here." Riley led him to the darkened bedroom, flipped on the overhead light, and pointed to the corner. "She doesn't seem to be able to get up."

He strode over and knelt at the dog's side. "What's the matter, little lady?" He offered her a sniff of the back of his fisted hand before scratching behind her ears. "Have you got trouble?"

She gave her tail a couple of weak thumps and licked his hand in greeting.

"You're right." He looked at Riley over his shoulder as he continued to stroke the dog's head. "Her breathing sounds weird. Let's get her to the vet and have her checked out."

Riley chewed her bottom lip as she wrung her hands. "We don't have a vet."

"No problem. I've got one in Corsicana."

She glanced at the illuminated face on the clock on the nightstand. "It's nine thirty. Will they be open?"

He nodded. "I called ahead and told her we might be coming. I'll text and confirm we're on our way, and she can meet us at the clinic."

For once she appreciated his high-handed, managing ways. "Oh. Okay."

Murmuring softly to the dog, he carefully scooped her up, bed and all. "You got room in the SUV, or should we take my truck?"

"We can take mine. It's empty." She led the way through the house to the garage. Sam pressed the garage door button with his elbow while she climbed in on the passenger side to fold down the rear seats.

She met him behind the vehicle and opened the hatch. "There should be plenty of room now."

Muscles bunching, Sam lowered the dog and bed onto the flat, carpeted surface, scooted it toward the center of the space, and stepped aside.

"Should I ride in the back with her?"

His arched brow and disapproving frown told her what he thought of the idea. He may be out of uniform, but he was still every inch a cop. "Not without a seat belt. The bolsters on the sides of her bed should keep her from rolling out. She'll be fine."

"Okay." She reached in to give Shadow a reassuring pat on the head. "Everything's going to be all right. You don't need to be afraid."

The dimple appeared in his cheek. "You talking to the dog?"

She'd said the same thing to him the day he brought Shadow to her. The memory made her smile. "Me? No. That would be weird."

He laughed. "Want me to drive?"

Knowing him, he intended to drive whether she wanted him to or not, but it was nice of him to make it sound as though she had a choice. "Yes. Let me lock up the house, and we'll go."

Minutes later they pulled out on the highway. Streetlights cast broad arcs of light on the darkened road. Traffic was sparse. "How far is Corsicana from here?"

"We'll be there in thirty minutes."

Suddenly aware of the magnitude of her imposition on this man she hardly knew, she shifted in her seat to face him. "I'm sorry I interrupted your Friday night. I hope I didn't mess up your plans."

"No problem." Brow lifted, he sent her a questioning glance. "I wasn't the one with the date."

"Date?" She frowned. "Oh, I did say I was out tonight, didn't I?" She shook her head. "It wasn't a date. I had dinner with Mary Jo."

The lights on the dash illuminated his smile. "Mary Jo and I go back a long way."

"I guess being a local, you go back a long way with most of the town."

Eyes on the road, he nodded. "True."

"Do you ever wish you could live someplace else?"

"Occasionally. But deep down, I know Village Green is where I belong. These are the people I'm called to serve."

Riley pondered his words for a moment. "You consider being a policeman a calling?"

He grinned. "I sure hope so. I'm pretty sure it's not about the money and glamour."

She'd never really thought about it before. Law enforcement was probably one of the most underpaid, overworked, and under-appreciated jobs. "No, I guess not. Do you think most people in law enforcement see it as a calling?"

"Yes. Obviously, I can't answer for everyone, but I believe the majority do." He glanced away from the road to look at her. "I've never known anyone to take such an interest in the psyche of a cop."

She shrugged. "Just making conversation."

He sent her a look of disbelief before returning his attention to the highway. "One day you're going to have to tell me about what-ever it was that put you off cops so bad."

"Maybe."

Shadow whimpered. Riley twisted around as far as she could in her seat belt. "It's okay, baby. We're almost there."

Sam pulled up in front of the single-story brick structure, flickered the headlights, and shut off the engine. "Here we are." He unstrapped his seat belt.

Riley climbed out of the vehicle and met him at the back bumper. "I can't thank you enough for this."

The front door of the clinic swung open, and Doc Sherrie stepped out. Dressed in a baggy T-shirt and jeans, with her dark hair pulled up on top of her head, it was obvious she was already into her weekend. "You made good time. I just got here. You know, you're really going to owe me."

Riley shot him a look of apology. "I'm sorry," she whispered. "I didn't mean to get you into trouble."

"I can handle her." He climbed into the back of the SUV and tugged the bed to the edge so he could get a better grip on it. The dog's breath came in short bursts. "It's okay, girl." He slid his arms underneath and lifted the dog and bed to his chest.

Riley lowered the hatch and locked it before hurrying behind him into the building.

"Doc Sherrie, this is Riley Vreeland and her dog, Shadow. Riley, this is Sherrie Roberts." Arms full, he made the introductions with nods.

"Hey, Riley." The doctor shot Riley a distracted smile, her full focus locked on the dog. "Let's get the patient into my exam room."

Sam and Sherrie walked side by side down the hall, Riley following closely on their heels.

"I'm really sorry we dragged you out on a Friday night," Riley said. "Something's the matter with Shadow, and I didn't know what to do, so I called Sam—"

Sherrie paused outside one of the rooms. "It's no problem. If my baby brother didn't get me out of bed at least once a month, I'd worry."

"Baby brother?" Riley looked from one to the other. "Sam's your brother?"

She grinned and nodded. "Yup. Four years younger."

Okay, he probably should have told her in advance. "What? You didn't figure cops had sisters?"

"Well, yes, I guess—"

"He's got two sisters. The other one lives in Dallas with her family." Sherrie stepped into the small, narrow room and switched on the overhead lights. "Put her on the table here."

Sam gently lowered the dog and bed onto the steel-topped platform, keeping a hand on the dog to keep her from falling.

"So, what brings you here today, pretty girl?" Humans forgotten, Sherrie crooned to the patient as her fingers gently probed through Shadow's soft fur. Her hands paused on the dog's abdomen. She tossed her head back and laughed. "Well, you vixen. I don't think you'll be able to keep your secret much longer."

"What secret?" Riley stood pressed to Sam's side as she watched the examination. "What's wrong?"

Sherrie grinned. "It appears our girl here has been stepping out with a gentleman caller."

At Riley's blank look she said, "Shadow is in labor."

Riley blinked. "She's going to have a baby?"

Sherrie nodded. "From the feel of things, I'd say several."

Jaw slack, Riley backed into one of the two chairs lined against the wall behind them and dropped. "I had no idea. I don't know much about dogs. I've only had her for a month or so. Sam found her and brought her to me." She stopped babbling to narrow her eyes at him. "Did you know she was pregnant?"

He lifted his shoulders in an apologetic shrug. "Not a clue. She was skin and bones when I found her."

His sister nodded. "The signs would have been easy to miss if she was undernourished. The average gestation period for a dog is about sixty-three days, so she was maybe halfway along when you picked her up."

Riley stood, a stricken expression on her face. "Poor little thing. I had no idea. She hasn't had any prenatal care."

"She looks great," Sherrie assured her. "Dogs are naturally resilient. They've been doing this in the wild for ages. She and the puppies will be fine."

"Puppies." Riley sat back down, palms pressed to her flushed cheeks. "Oh my gosh, I'm going to have puppies."

Sherrie laughed as she pulled on a pair of disposable gloves from a box hanging on the back of the door. "Stand there at her head with Sam and talk to her while I do an exam to see where we are in the process."

Obediently, Riley moved to his side. "First fleas and worms, now puppies." She didn't sound mad, simply dazed. "The gift that keeps on giving."

Oh, man. When he'd presented her with the dog, he'd meant to provide her with a companion. As in one. A pal, not a pack. "I guess I owe you an apology."

"No way." She smiled gently as she stroked the dog's neck. "Shadow is wonderful, and I wouldn't change a thing. Well, maybe the worms . . ." Her gaze sharpened as she looked up into his eyes. "But you are about to take a much more active role. I know even less about baby dogs than I do about grown ones."

"I'll be glad to help." It'd be interesting to see how that played out. She'd made it clear she didn't want him around, that she tolerated him for the sake of her students. So maybe she'd have the puppies one weekend, then he'd have them the next? "We'll figure it out."

Sherrie pulled off the gloves and tossed them into the trash. "First puppy is in the birth canal. We should have him or her within the hour."

For all his experience with dogs, he didn't know much about the delivery process. "That long?"

Sherrie nodded. "I anticipate we'll be here all night. Once we see how Shadow does with the first one, I may disappear for a nap."

"You're not leaving us?" Riley sounded panicked.

He felt like Riley sounded. "Uh, Sher, we're going to want you to stick around."

Sherrie laughed. "There's a cot in my office. I'll be just down the hall. But I doubt you'll need me. Dogs take care of this by themselves."

She nodded to Sam. "Help me grab some bedding and towels to make our little mother more comfortable. Riley, keep a hand on her to prevent her from standing until we get back."

Riley's eyes, more blue than green tonight, widened as she nodded. "Hurry back."

Sam followed his sister down the hall to the supply room that smelled of clean sheets and disinfectant. She switched on the light and started pulling linens off the shelf and stacking them in his arms.

"Way to go, little brother. She's a real beauty."

"Are we talking human or dog?"

She paused long enough to slug him in the arm. "You're a regular riot, you know that? I'm talking about Riley. She seems nice. And classy. I really like her."

"She's a friend. That's all."

Sherrie huffed out a breath as she scooped a couple more towels off the shelf. "Do you know what your problem is? You know a million great women, but they're all just friends."

He lifted his shoulders. "I can't help that I'm a friendly guy."

She snorted. "I don't think you notice when a woman is interested in you."

"Maybe, but I definitely notice when they're not. Riley seems to have a thing about cops."

She added the towels to the stack in his arms. "Define *thing*."

"Trust issues."

"You should have been a lawyer like Dad."

This wasn't the first time he'd heard that. "Yuh, like anyone trusts lawyers. Besides, I like being a cop."

Dark eyes similar to his own locked onto his. "Then make her like it too. I'm telling you, Sam, this one's a keeper."

Riley's face lit with relief when they returned to the exam room. "Thank goodness, you're back. She seems to be breathing harder."

"Good sign." Sherrie spread out a small canvas tarp in the corner of the room and topped it with six or seven towels. "Sam, would you put Shadow and the bed here? This will give her more space in case she wants to move around during the delivery."

Once again, he scooped up the dog and bed and carried them to the whelping area in the corner, gently placing them against the wall. The look of trust in the dog's eyes mirrored the one he'd seen in her owner's eyes when he first arrived at her house tonight. It contained both a plea for help and the settled belief he would give it. Their confidence in him was both empowering and humbling. "Okay, little momma, it's up to you now. If you need anything, remember we're here for you."

"We'll give her some privacy." Sherrie dimmed the lights. "We may as well get comfortable. This is going to take a while."

Riley looked up at him. "Do you need to leave?" It sounded like she wanted him to stay.

"And miss this? No way." He pointed toward the wall. "You two can have the chairs."

She shook her head. "No, I'm good. You sit with your sister."

The look he gave her was a mix of horror and disbelief. "I hope my mother raised me better than that. You sit by Sherrie; I'll go get us all something cold to drink."

"None for me, thanks." Riley shook her head. "I don't think I could drink anything."

"Everything's going to be fine," Sherrie assured her. "Sam, why don't you lead us in a prayer for peace and a safe delivery?"

Hands clasped, they bowed their heads as he prayed.

Puppy number one, a sleek black female, arrived at 10:37. Sherrie stood by to assist, but Shadow seemed to know exactly what to do. Riley paced the tiny room.

After they'd admired the new arrival, his sister excused herself with a massive yawn. "That girl's got it, and this girl is beat. I'm going down to my office for a nap. Call me if you need anything. I'll set my phone to wake me in two hours."

She was right. He owed her *big* time. "Thanks for everything, Sher. Have a good rest."

Puppy number two arrived an hour later. Once again, Shadow took care of the details while he observed, and Riley paced.

When things quieted down, he patted the chair beside his. "Come sit. Take a break."

"Maybe just for a second." She made one more pass by the dogs, cooing her encouragement, before dropping down on the chair with a weary sigh. "I don't want Shadow to think she's in this alone."

He glanced toward the corner. "She seems pretty chill. Now that she's got those puppies licked clean, maybe she'll rest if you do."

Her gaze remained on the dogs. "I'm really proud of her."

"She's going to be a great momma." It sounded crazy, but witnessing firsthand the whole noisy, messy struggle to bring life into the world had felt as though he'd been a part of something almost sacred. "After tonight, my appreciation for females, of any species, is at an all-time high."

They lapsed into a comfortable silence in the semidarkness. Shadow's breathing slowed as she regained strength for the next round. The two puppies squirmed and squeaked at her side.

"I wonder how many she'll have." Riley's whisper sounded sleepy.

"Good question."

She yawned. "I'm glad she's not a dalmatian."

He turned his head slightly. "Why's that?"

"I don't know what the Coopers would say about a hundred and one puppies." The first-grade level joke sent the woman he'd characterized as focused and levelheaded into breathless giggles.

Poor kid was punchy. "Why don't you try to catch a few z's. I'll wake you when things start to happen."

Her laughter subsided and she shook her head. "I couldn't leave. Besides, I doubt your sister has two cots."

"Stay here. You can lean on me."

The look she gave him, more assessment than outrage, brought a smile to his face. He cocked his head toward the door. "My sister is right down the hall."

She rolled her eyes. "I wasn't worried about my virtue. I just hate to be a bother."

"Serve and protect," he reminded her as he leaned against the hard-backed, plastic chair and tapped his shoulder.

To his surprise, she complied. She scooted into the curve of her seat and gently rested her head against his upper arm. "I won't be able to sleep, but it'll be nice to close my eyes for a moment."

Her hair smelled great. Clean and flowery. She must have ordered more of that high-dollar shampoo. She shifted once or twice, apparently trying to find a comfortable spot, then settled. In no time, her breathing slowed, and her head grew heavy on his shoulder.

He smiled. She-who-wouldn't-be-able-to-sleep was out like a light.

A slightly disheveled Sherrie walked into the exam room about 12:45. She glanced over at him and grinned. "You and your *friend* look cozy," she whispered.

"Don't get any ideas." He directed his words to both his sister and himself. It was an uphill battle not to weave fantasies while sitting in the dark and holding a sweet-smelling woman in his arms. And she was literally in his arms.

As her body relaxed in sleep, she'd begun to slump forward. To keep her from falling to the floor, he slid his arm behind her, anchoring her to his chest, her ear pressed to his heart.

He couldn't begin to explain why it felt so right.

"You get any sleep?" he whispered.

She nodded. "Yeah. How 'bout you?"

Careful not to disturb Riley, he shook his head. "It's my watch."

She smiled. "Forget what I said about you being a lawyer. You're a cop down to your chromosomes." She glanced toward the corner. "How's our patient?"

"Things seem to be ramping up again. I don't know how she can do all that with babies pestering her."

"The question of mothers everywhere." She crossed to the pallet. Squatting down, she clicked on her penlight. After a minute or two of examination, she turned it off and returned to his side. "Third one's almost here. Momma seems strong. Puppies look good."

"How many more you think we've got?"

"One or two at the most." She studied him for a moment. "I've got my second wind, so I'll take the next watch. Why don't you try to grab a little shut-eye."

"Thanks." He closed his gritty eyes and let his head fall back to rest against the wall. He inhaled deeply, saturating himself in Riley's fragrance, and slept.

# CHAPTER SIX

E yes closed, Riley came awake in slow stages. By degrees, she
ascertained that half of her was sitting on a hard chair while the
other half was draped over something wonderfully warm, her cheek
resting on a firm, cottony surface. Her head nestled comfortably,
she arched her spine in an indulgent stretch and sighed.

"Good morning, sleepyhead."

Sam! Her eyes shot wide as she planted her hands on what she
now realized was his chest and shoved herself into an upright position on her own chair. "I am *so* sorry. I didn't mean to fall asleep."
Disorientation mixed with acute embarrassment. She pushed her
hair off her face and squinted at him. "What time is it?"

Sam checked his watch. "Five forty-five."

"Oh my gosh! I've been asleep for hours." She sprang to her
feet. "How's Shadow?"

He pointed toward the whelping area. "Mother and puppies are
in excellent health and resting comfortably."

"Is it over?" She tiptoed toward the dogs in an attempt not to
disturb them. "How many?"

"Four. Three girls and a boy."

Shadow's tail thumped as Riley stood over her. Four sleek black
bodies lay in a tangle at her side. "Congratulations, little momma.
What a brave girl you've been."

She surveyed the area as she crouched to scratch Shadow behind the ears. "Everything looks cleaner."

"My sister's touch. She was here for the last two deliveries and helped Shadow tidy up when it was done."

Riley glanced around. "Where is Sherrie now?"

"Sleeping."

She straightened and turned to face him. "What about you? Did you get any sleep?"

He nodded. "Sherrie spotted me a couple hours."

Guilt twisted the corners of her mouth. "I'm really sorry. It's my dog, and I was no help."

He shook his head. "Everybody took a turn. Since they're going home with you, I'd say your contribution will be the biggest."

"Going home with me?" Her voice ended on a squeak. Honestly, with all the excitement, she hadn't thought that far in advance. All the new babies she was acquainted with spent several days in the hospital. "When?"

"This morning. My sister checked them all out and pronounced them ready to release."

A nasty shot of adrenaline electrified her nerve endings. "I don't know anything about puppies."

"Shadow does." His smile was gentle, his voice low and calming. "And Sherrie will send you home with detailed instructions. Don't worry, you've got this."

Good thing one of them thought so.

A too-short hour later, they waved goodbye to Sherrie as they pulled out of the clinic parking lot, Shadow and puppies snuggled into a towel-lined veterinary supply box in the back.

Riley lowered her hand as they pulled out of sight. "Your sister is amazing."

"You sound surprised."

"Impressed." She glanced over at him and frowned. "She wouldn't let me pay her. I tried every way I knew to convince her, but she flat refused. She insisted Shadow did all the work."

He grinned as he shook his head. "You never know about Sherrie. She sometimes does that for my friends."

An unpleasant thought forced its way into the warm cocoon that seemed to envelop them since sharing in such a miraculous event, the cozy sense that the two of them were somehow alone and specially connected.

*Just how many women has he given strays to?*

He'd known just what to do when she called in a panic last night. Was that from much practice? Was this a regular thing for him, spending the night at the clinic with a woman sleeping on him?

If so, why in the world did it feel as though he'd been unfaithful?

She turned slightly in her seat so she could surreptitiously study him out of the corner of her eye. The weak, early light framed his head, accentuating his profile.

Had she thought him boyish? How had she missed the strong lines of his face, the set of his brow and chin? The stubble on his cheeks emphasized the chiseled contours. Sam Walker, her all-American good guy, was all man.

Not that he was hers. Not by any stretch of the imagination. The last twelve hours had created a false sense of intimacy and connection between them. It probably happened to him all the time—undoubtedly there was a well-documented syndrome in which a civilian bonded with their law enforcement rescuer.

"After I drop you off—"

"Drop me off?" Panic sounded in her voice. "You're not staying?" Syndrome or not, she wasn't ready to go it alone.

He scrubbed a hand over his face. "I need to run by my place and get cleaned up. Maybe grab a few more hours of sleep."

Poor man had to be dead on his feet. "Of course. Are you working today?"

He shook his head. "I've got the weekend off. If it's okay with you, I'll stop by your place this afternoon, just to check on you and the gang."

"It's better than okay." Was he kidding? She'd organize a week-long festival just to keep him nearby. "If you're able, plan to stay for dinner and we'll celebrate."

He looked over at her in surprise. "You cook?"

She didn't want to get his hopes up by overselling her skills. "It's probably more accurate to say I get by."

"Works for me. Thanks. I'll be there."

It was a testimony to her apprehension of being left alone with the dogs that she unlocked the door and entered the house without her usual precautions. Of course, it might also have something to do with the two hundred pounds of muscle following two steps behind her.

"Where should we put them?"

*Good question.* She flipped on the lights in the kitchen. "Your sister suggested I put them someplace out of the way so they can have privacy. She warned me that things would get noisy as the puppies got older, so my bedroom is out."

"Let's put them in the one next to yours." He sidestepped her and headed down the hall. "Grab a couple towels to put under the box, would you?"

She paused outside the bathroom door. "Towels?"

He grinned. "There *will* be moisture."

"Oh." *Ewww.*

She pulled several fluffy green ones from the linen closet and, entering the bedroom behind him, spread them over the floor. "I'll need to go towel shopping for the Coopers when this is over."

Sam gently lowered the cardboard box onto the towels. "Home sweet home."

Arms folded across her middle, Riley studied the makeshift housing. "That box isn't going to last very long."

Nodding, he took up the position beside her. "You'll need something waterproof with sides high enough so the puppies can't escape."

She chewed her bottom lip. "Maybe Mr. Buchanan at the hardware store has something."

"Let me take care of it. A gift for the new mother."

She lifted her gaze to his. "Are you sure?"

"Positive." He glanced down at the dogs before looking over at her. "If you're good, I'll take off."

Her stomach knotted. "And if I'm not good?"

He laughed as though she were joking. Which she definitely was not. "You've got this."

The strangest urge to cry came over her. "I don't know where to begin thanking you for everything you've done." Unshed tears clogged her throat.

"It was my pleasure." He chucked her under the chin. "And don't worry. You're going to be just fine."

A tear escaped and trailed down her cheek as she locked the door behind him.

Her footfalls echoed on the hardwood when she retraced her steps to the puppies. She hadn't felt this alone since her dad died. Because he'd been sick for a while, and she'd buried her mother the year before, she'd been somewhat prepared for the grief. What she hadn't expected was the sense of abandonment. He was her last living relative. With his final breath, she became an orphan.

As she sat on the edge of the bed and stared into the box, that same sensation, the overwhelming feeling that everything now depended on her, welled up. She wrapped her arms around her middle and wept.

Blinded by misery, she didn't notice Shadow had climbed out of her box until the dog leaned her warm side against Riley's leg. She slid off the bed to pull her close, and Shadow licked her chin.

Riley smiled through the tears. "Technically, I should be comforting you."

The dog thumped her tail.

She rested her cheek on the dog's head. "I'm afraid I don't have much to give. In the spirit of full disclosure, you should know I don't know the first thing about puppies."

Her cell phone rang, and she dug it out of her pocket. Mary Jo.

Oh mercy, they were supposed to meet this morning. "Hey, Mary Jo. I'm glad you called." She sniffled. "I've had a crazy night. Shadow had puppies, so I won't be able to walk with you today."

"Puppies? Really? Now that's what I call an unexpected blessing!" *Count on Mary Jo to see the upside in everything.* "I've already got my sneakers on. Would it be okay if I came over to take a peek?"

Riley swiped at her wet face with her sleeve. "Well . . . okay. I warn you, I'm a wreck. I haven't washed my face or brushed my hair, and I'm still wearing the clothes I wore when I saw you last night."

"You'll look lovely to me. I'll be over in a few."

Riley had time to brush her teeth and hair before Mary Jo arrived.

After running through her security ritual and determining the person on her porch was her elderly neighbor wearing a hot pink track suit, she unlocked the front and screen doors and ushered her in.

Mary Jo lifted the white bakery bag she carried. "Joe dropped off some of Eden's pumpkin muffins this morning."

Riley nodded. She hadn't met Joe or Eden, but she knew Mary Jo thought of them as family and spoke of them often.

"They'll be the perfect thing to celebrate the new arrivals."

Riley's stomach growled. "Sounds delicious. I haven't made tea yet."

She laughed. "When would you have had the time? Why don't you have a seat in the kitchen, and I'll brew us a pot? We'll have a nice breakfast, then send you off to bed for a nap."

Riley shook her head. "The eating part sounds amazing, but I couldn't sleep. I need to keep an eye on Shadow and the puppies to be sure everything is okay."

Mary Jo looped an arm through hers and escorted her to the kitchen. "Lucky for you, I've always wanted the opportunity to dog sit. My sweet husband was allergic to dogs, so we never had one of our own. You can have a rest, and I can enjoy watching the puppies."

Riley dug tea bags out of the pantry while Mary Jo filled the kettle and turned on the stove. Shadow trotted into the room to investigate.

"Here's our little momma now." Her neighbor bent to stroke the dog's head. "I can't wait to hear all about your exciting night."

Over a cup of hot tea and the best pumpkin muffin she'd ever tasted, Riley related the details as best she could.

"What an adventure! And you never suspected a thing?" Mary Jo snuck a chunk of muffin under the table to the dog.

Now that the excitement had passed, Riley felt pretty stupid admitting the dog's imminent delivery caught her by complete surprise. "Not a clue. Poor thing. It breaks my heart to think about Shadow's life before Sam found her, pregnant and out there all by herself."

Mary Jo's smile was partially hidden by the porcelain cup she held to her lips. "Isn't it just like God in His mercy to bring her here, to you, to love and care for?"

"He probably should have given her to someone with a little more experience." She lifted her gaze to her friend. "I'm terrified something will go wrong."

Mary Jo frowned. "Did the veterinarian give any indication that you should be concerned?"

She took a sip of tea. "Well, no. She thinks Shadow can handle it."

"Dr. Roberts is a very wise young woman." She slipped another bite of muffin beneath the table. "I'm confident everything will be fine, and I know if a need arises, God will show you what to do, just like He did last night when you thought to call Sam."

Her simple confidence was both inspiring and convicting. Riley placed her cup on its saucer and sent her friend a smile. "Mary Jo, I hope one day I'll see things the way you do."

"What way is that?"

"You seem to process everything through . . . a God filter."

The older woman laughed. "Trust me, I fall short so often. But I've learned that each time He stretches us, He's giving us the opportunity to trust Him and see His mighty hand at work. The key is to cling to His promise that He'll never leave or forsake us."

Riley absorbed this. When was the last time she'd reminded herself of God's promised care? Sometime before she'd gone into hiding. Recently, she'd been acting as though everything depended on her. She'd let fear overshadow her faith.

"Yup. I want to be just like you when I grow up." She covered a yawn with her hand. "Excuse me."

Mary Jo stood. "Time for bed. Once I clear up these few dishes, I'll take sentry duty."

She shook her head. "No, I can't let—"

"I insist. Off you go." She motioned her away with a sweep of her hands. "Shadow will show me where the babies are."

Physical and mental exhaustion rolled over Riley like a wave, and suddenly she could hardly keep her eyes open. She yawned again. "Okay, but only for a little while. I promise I won't sleep long."

Expression fierce, Mary Jo clapped her hands on her hips. "If I see you in less than two hours, there will be trouble."

Riley laughed. "Thank you."

Her neighbor picked up their plates and carried them to the sink, Shadow following closely on her heels. "You're welcome, dear one. Sleep well."

Sam pulled up behind the dual cab pickup parked in front of Riley's. What was Joe Wolfe doing here? He gathered the bouquet and stack of newspapers off the passenger seat and strode to the front door.

Joe answered his knock. "Hey, man, come in."

Sam walked inside, past Joe, and placed the newspapers on the corner of the dining room table. "What are you doing here?"

"Same thing as you, I imagine. Eden and Jake and I came to see the new puppies. Mary Jo called us, and we brought over some food. Riley's been asleep, but she's in the shower now." He eyed the bundle in Sam's hands. "Gotta admit, I didn't think to bring flowers. Honestly, I didn't know dogs were into that sort of thing."

"Ha ha." Sam cuffed him on the shoulder. "The flowers are for Riley, idiot."

Joe's brows climbed to his hairline, and a wide grin split his face. "It's like that, is it?"

Oh, man. Why hadn't he left them in the car? He kept his expression neutral. "Like what?"

"You. Riley. Flowers."

Sam rolled his eyes. "No, it's not like that. Just because you're a newlywed doesn't mean the rest of us are operating under the influence of Cupid. Riley and I are just friends. That's all."

His childhood buddy adopted a wounded expression. "You and I are friends, and you never give me flowers."

Sam had to bite back a grin. "No, but I'm about to give you a black eye."

Just then Eden came around the corner from the back of the house. "Hi, Sam." She gave him a quick hug then slipped her hand into Joe's. "Why are you threatening my husband?"

*Where to begin?* "Because he's a knucklehead."

When she looked to Joe for clarification, he gave her an innocent shrug before pulling her close. "I just asked him about his relationship with Riley, and he got all touchy." He whispered loudly enough for Sam to hear. "You know the old expression, where there's smoke, there's fire. Just saying."

Eden turned to Sam with an expression of delight. "Are you and Riley—"

"Friends." He said it with what he hoped was enough finality to nip this in the bud. No pun intended. "We're friends."

"Friends with flowers," Joe amended.

Sam gave him a side-eyed look. "Man, I'm going to have to hurt you."

"Sam, there's no shame in you having a thing for Riley." Eyes dancing, Eden clearly enjoyed his discomfort.

He glared at Joe. "Since I can't hurt her, I'm going to have to hurt you worse."

Riley padded into the room on bare feet, wearing jeans and a blue T-shirt, a white towel wrapped around her head like a turban. He was happy to see her expression brighten when she noticed him. "Hi, Sam. Why are you threatening people in my home?"

Darn. He had hoped she hadn't overhead them. Since there was no good way to answer her question without getting into territory he didn't want to cover, he ignored it.

Stepping toward her, he scanned her face. She looked better. Rested. Even relaxed. "How's it going? Did you get some sleep?"

She nodded. "A couple of hours. Mary Jo brought over muffins earlier, then these beautiful people brought some of Eden's amazing coffee cake, so I'm rested and well fed."

"Beautiful people" was disgustingly accurate. Both Joe and his wife were movie star attractive. As much as he'd like to, Sam couldn't hold it against them because they were also his good friends.

Riley looked from Eden to Joe. "You have no idea how great it is to finally meet you and put faces to names. I feel I know both of you already since Mary Jo talks about you often. I'm easily five pounds heavier because of your bakery, Eden." She glanced over her shoulder toward the hall she'd just come from. "And your son Jake is adorable."

Eden smiled. "I hope you don't mind us stopping by. When we heard there were puppies, we couldn't resist."

"I'm glad you came. Jake's very sweet with Shadow."

"We told him he couldn't touch the puppies yet," Joe said. "He'll have to wait until they're older."

"I hope you'll bring him by often. It'll be a great way for him to learn about animals and for them to learn about people."

"Spoken like a true educator." Mary Jo appeared from around the corner with Jake in her arms. "Hello, Sam. Shadow and her babies are having a nap, so we decided to give them some quiet."

He bent to kiss her cheek. "Hey, Mary Jo. This is quite a party."

"Everyone was so excited about the big news." She beamed up at him. "Thank you for taking such good care of the girls last night."

He shrugged. "My sister gets the credit."

Riley shook her head. "Don't let him kid you. It was a team effort. The two of them totally saved the day."

When her gaze fell on the cellophane-wrapped flowers he carried, he had no choice but to hand them to her in front of the eager audience. "Oh, yeah." He shoved the bundle toward her. "I, uh, brought these."

Could he be any more awkward? And in front of witnesses?

Accepting the bouquet, she tipped her gaze to his, a question in her eyes. "Are these for Shadow or me?"

Joe shot him a grin before guffawing. "A valid question. We were discussing that very thing before you joined us. Do dogs *like* flowers?"

He'd never hear the end of it. "The flowers are for you."

"Thank you. That's really sweet." She favored him with a big smile before heading toward the kitchen. "Let me get them in water."

"I guess we should be going," Eden said. "It's time for lunch and naps." She turned to Sam. "We're doing dinner at our place tonight. Mary Jo's coming. We'd love for you to join us."

"Thanks, but Riley invited me to eat here."

She smiled. "I meant for you to bring her along. We have plenty."

"No!" Joe and Mary Jo spoke in unison.

"I know Riley said she wanted to stay close to home for a couple of days." Mary Jo's hurried explanation was an obvious attempt to cover up her outburst. "To keep an eye on the puppies. Sam can keep her company tonight, and we'll all get together for dinner . . . another time."

"Good plan." Joe took Jake from Mary Jo's arms. "We'll take off so . . . uh . . . so the puppies can have some quiet." He placed his free hand on Eden's shoulder, herding her toward the door.

Sans turban, hair hanging in damp waves at her shoulders, Riley returned from the kitchen as they were poised to leave. She frowned. "Are you going already?"

"Yes, dear, I'm afraid we must." Mary Jo avoided Riley's eyes as she made her explanation. "Eden and Joe need to get Jake down for his nap, and I, uh, I have a Sunday school lesson to prepare."

"Oh, well, thank you for coming this morning and for bringing breakfast. Between the food, nap, and shower, I feel like a new person." Riley hugged her before turning to the others with a broad smile. "It was a pleasure to finally meet you. And thank you again for the coffee cake. It is amazing. I meant it when I said I'd love for you to bring Jake back to visit the dogs. I'm here most afternoons and weekends."

Joe smiled. "It was great to meet you, and we'll be back."

Riley stood at Sam's side in the doorway to watch them hustle away. "I'm sorry they rushed off. I hope they didn't think they weren't welcome to stay."

"No, it wasn't that." It was the most flagrant attempt at matchmaking he'd ever witnessed. Ordinarily it took half an hour for everyone to say their goodbyes and give their round of hugs. Today, they pulled away from the curb in under five minutes. A new record. He'd almost laughed to see them hotfooting out of the house and across the yard to the truck, as though the hounds of hell pursued them.

Too bad their efforts were wasted. He and Riley were just friends. Or more accurately, working toward friendship.

Once they were out of sight, she turned to him. "Thank you for coming. Did you get any rest?"

He shook his head. "I grabbed a shower, but I was too busy to sleep. Wait till you see what I got." He pushed open the storm door, dashed across the front lawn, and retrieved the blue plastic baby pool he'd stashed in the back of the truck. Carrying it across his chest like a shield, he sprinted back to the house, turning sideways to fit through the door.

She studied it with a baffled frown. "A pool?"

"Maybe to the uninitiated, but to those in the know it's a deluxe dog bed and puppy corral."

Understanding dawned on her face and she bobbed her head. "I get it. It's plastic for easy cleanup, and the babies can't get over the sides."

"Exactly. Do you have any idea how hard it is to find a kiddie pool at the end of September?"

She stepped around him to lock the door. "I can honestly say I've never thought about it. I take it you had a tough time."

"I've been to every Walmart between here and Fort Worth before I snagged one." He waited until he had her attention before tapping the rim. "This baby is solid gold."

She laughed. "We'll treasure it."

"I also rounded up all the newspapers I could find, probably enough to last a month. I put them on the table in there."

Riley preceded him into the dining room. "Do the puppies stay in the pool that long?"

He hiked up his shoulders. "Beats me. I guess we'll find out, right?"

She picked up the stack of papers and hugged them to her chest. "I really appreciate this. The papers and pool certainly, but also the fact you're spending your day off to help me."

She wanted to spend time with him. *This was a first.* "That's what friends are for. Besides, I managed to wrangle dinner out of the deal. Seems like a fair trade."

"I hope you feel the same way after you taste my cooking." She glanced at the pool dangling from his fingers. "Should we go ahead and transfer everybody to their new bed?"

"I'm ready if you are." He led the way, careful not to hit the walls as he traveled down the hall.

Shadow sat up and thumped her tail when he stepped into the bedroom. He laid the pool on the floor and crouched at her side. "Hey, little momma." He kept his voice low. "How's it going?"

"She's had a big morning. After eating most of the bowl of food I put out for her and at least half of Mary Jo's pumpkin muffin, she had some alone time in the yard before her guests arrived."

"How's she doing with the puppies?"

Riley shrugged. "Good, I guess. She gets out of the box occasionally but doesn't stay away long. Your sister said the puppies should eat every two hours and from what I can tell, they eat constantly. Hard to know what's going on, but they seem to be attached like Sherrie said they should."

"You're doing great." He petted the dog as he praised her. "Best mom ever."

She lifted liquid brown eyes to his, and her expression once again mirrored the one in her owner's eyes this morning. The apprehension and worry from the night before had been replaced by a contented peace.

"Okay, Shadow, we're going to move you and the kids to your new digs. Not only will your family have additional space to grow in, but things will be more hygienic as well."

The dog watched his face, head tilted, clearly listening.

"Hold on while I slide the box to the side here." He gently scooted the cardboard box out of the corner and set the pool in its place.

Riley lined the bottom with several layers of newspaper. "Ready."

He reached for the first puppy, and Shadow growled a low warning. Surprised, he pulled his hands back, palms out. "My fault. Moving too fast."

He sat back on his haunches and spoke quietly. "If it's all right with you, I'm going to move your puppies. I won't hurt them, I promise."

He kept up a steady flow of soft-spoken chatter while he reached toward the one on the end and carefully picked it up, transferring it to the clean newspaper. Shadow watched the painstakingly slow process closely but didn't protest. When everybody had been moved, she stepped daintily into the plastic tub and, after inspecting her children, she lay down beside them with a sigh.

Riley blew out a breath. "Whew. That was unexpectedly nerve-racking. I felt like I was watching delicate surgery."

"You're telling me. I felt like the surgeon performing it." The transfer had been surprisingly intense, the success of the mission based solely on trust.

"They're really sweet, aren't they?" Riley sat at the foot of the double bed.

The mattress dipped as he took the place beside her. "I wonder what they'll look like. I guess a lot of it depends on their father."

"I hope they don't look anything like him." She stiffened, her answer surprisingly fierce. "A man who would force himself on a woman alone doesn't deserve any place in her life."

Stunned by her vehemence, he turned to stare at her. "Are we still talking about dogs?"

Her gaze glanced off his before settling on the litter. "What? Oh, sure. I just hate to think of Shadow being preyed upon when she was so vulnerable."

Instead of going with his initial response and reminding her that both dogs had likely been guided by deeply ingrained instinct, he chose to be silent. A good cop knew most people were uncomfortable in extended silence and would talk to fill it. These quiet moments often produced the deepest insight.

When five minutes had passed, he knew that particular window of opportunity had closed. No matter. He could be patient. As with moving the puppies, the success of his mission to understand Riley was based on his ability to earn her trust. And trust took time.

Dinner offered no further glimpses into the mystery of his hostess, although he did discover she made a surprisingly delicious stir fry.

"That was fantastic." He pulled his napkin from his lap and placed it on the table beside his plate. "You're a really good cook."

Cheeks flushed, she accepted the compliment with a modest dip of her chin. "Thank you. I don't get much practice. It never seems worth it when I'm cooking for myself, but I have a couple of specialties I can pull out in a pinch." She sent him a smile across the table. "At the risk of bragging, I make a pretty mean lasagna."

"I have a major weakness for Italian food. Especially lasagna."

She stood to gather their plates. "I'll make it for you sometime."

Now here was progress. Before this weekend, she'd actively pushed him away. Since Shadow's delivery, Riley seemed to be softening toward him.

Tonight's casual invitation to a future dinner confirmed the change. Realistically, he didn't envision himself as a frequent guest at her table, but it was an encouraging sign. He'd known from the moment he'd met her that she needed a friend, but until now he'd never entertained the possibility he would be the one to fill that role. Or that friendship would hold so much appeal.

# CHAPTER SEVEN

Riley walked along the row of desks, collecting the letters from her students. "I'll take these to the post office today and send them off to Mrs. Cooper. I know she will be cheered up when she sees them."

"Do you think she's sad?"

She stopped to smile into Justin's upturned, worried face. She loved the empathy of first graders. "Maybe a little. And tired too. Mrs. Cooper is very sick and that feels bad. Your letters and drawings will help her feel better."

He nodded. "I'd be sad if I didn't have any hair."

Mrs. Cooper had included a recent picture with her last letter, bravely exposing her newly bald head. They'd talked about it in class, that one of the effects of her treatment would be losing her hair.

"Miss Vreeland says it'll grow back," Olivia reminded them.

"I drew a picture of Shadow's puppies," Noah said. "That will make her happy."

Always on the lookout for teaching opportunities, Riley had incorporated her adoption of Shadow into their lessons. They'd discussed taking responsibilities for a pet, and with the surprise addition of puppies last week, their lessons had expanded to include a study of baby animals.

Shadow now had her own bulletin board, edged with colorful cardboard cutouts of dog bones that Riley updated almost daily. Once Dr. Sherrie declared them old enough, Riley planned to bring the whole brood to school for a special show-and-tell.

In the spirit of full disclosure, she kept her landlords in the canine loop as well. Though they'd graciously allowed her to keep Shadow when pets were not specified in the lease, she feared they'd be less willing to accept a pool full of puppies. Sam had assured her they'd be great about it, but she wasn't too sure.

Feeling the news was too weighty to be handled through texts, she'd telephoned them Saturday night after dinner, while Sam was still there for moral support. With the Coopers on speakerphone, she and Sam took turns relating the whole story, beginning with her frantic call to Sam and ending with mother and four puppies in a blue plastic swimming pool stashed in the guest bedroom.

The Coopers laughed through the entire tale, expressing their desire to have been there to experience the adventure firsthand and their delight in the surprise delivery of four healthy puppies. Their only stipulation to the additional occupants was that they receive regular updates and pictures.

The bell rang. "Okay, everybody, grab your lunches if you brought them and line up. It's time to head to the cafeteria. When we get back to the classroom after recess, Officer Sam will be here to read to us. Chris, you're our line leader today."

He accepted the much-coveted title with a dutiful nod. "Yes, ma'am." He collected his lunch from the cubby on the back wall and moved slowly to the head of the line.

She watched his lackluster reaction with concern. Ordinarily, he'd be over the moon with the honor and bouncing to the door.

Something was off with him, had been for the last week or so, but Riley couldn't put her finger on the problem. He was still the model student, attentive and engaged, but he didn't seem as enthusiastic. It was as if something repressed the joyous energy usually spilling from the little boy.

His clothes were clean, he had a new pair of sneakers, and his lunches were back to their original generous proportions, so whatever his mother was dealing with must have been resolved. He appeared to be healthy. Maybe it was just a phase.

Once all twenty fidgety bodies fitted themselves into a first grader's approximation of a line and Riley had pressed a finger to her lips to remind them to walk quietly in the hall, she nodded to Chris to lead them out. When the last student stepped from the room, she shut off the lights and pulled the door closed. She followed the parade into the cafeteria, making certain each child made it to their assigned table or the hot lunch line. With a nod to the teacher on lunchroom duty, she stepped into the hall and made a dignified beeline to the teachers' lounge.

Situated in the center of the building for common access for all staff, the lounge was an oasis of tranquility. Framed prints in peaceful colors hung on creamy white walls. Throw rugs echoing the colors in the artwork warmed the space and offered additional insulation from the activity in the halls. The heavy door swung closed behind her, separating her from the noise and bustle.

Riley had the room to herself. Retrieving her makeup bag from the bank of lockers, she ducked into the first of two restrooms. She flipped on the lights, a frame of round glass globes that surrounded the mirror like a Hollywood dressing room, and got to work. She had thirty minutes before she collected her kids from the cafeteria and escorted them outside for recess. Luckily, she didn't have playground duty this week. The first week of October heat would melt off any makeup she applied.

Turning her head from side to side, she studied her reflection. Not bad. Knowing she'd see Sam, she'd spent extra time on her hair and makeup. They'd spoken on the phone half a dozen times in the week since they brought the puppies home, but she hadn't seen him face-to-face. Since she'd been sleep-deprived and stressed-out the last time they were together, today she wanted to look her best.

She touched up her blush, powdered away the shine on her nose, and reapplied lip gloss. After brushing her hair, she took one final look, packed up her cosmetics, and stepped out of the restroom.

"Oh, hey girl! I didn't know you were in there." Sara Kelley, the other first-grade teacher, sat at the long rectangular table with her customary salad. She waved her over. "Come sit with me."

Riley slid into the chair across from her, makeup bag hidden in her lap.

"Where's your lunch?"

Riley nodded toward the door. "I've got a protein bar back in the room."

Sara rolled her eyes. "That's just gross." She frowned. "Actually, I wish I could eat those things and not feel like I'm being punished—then I'd be skinny like you, right?"

Riley snorted. "You look great, and you know it."

Suddenly alert, like a hound on a scent, her coworker put down her fork and gave Riley a thorough inspection. "What are you all gussied up about?"

Riley felt her face heat. "I'm not—"

"Girl, wearing a dress to work, especially one you had to iron, is the pinnacle of gussied up."

Knowing she was guilty as charged, she decided to address the lesser offense. "How do you know I ironed it?"

Another eye roll. "Puhlease. I don't have to own an iron to recognize the effects." She narrowed her gaze, studying Riley's face while she plumbed the mystery. "So, what's going on . . . Aha! Officer Hunky is coming today, isn't he? My class is ecstatic."

*Officer Hunky?* Riley lifted her shoulders and ducked her head. "Sam *is* coming, but—"

Sara batted a dismissive hand before digging into her salad. "Don't be embarrassed. Everybody's got a crush on him. I'm happily married with three kids, and *I've* got a crush on him."

"I don't have a crush on him." *Maybe a small one.*

"Well, you should." She forked a mound of lettuce into her mouth. "He's a great guy." She lifted her gaze. "Have I ever told you my method for determining if a guy is the real deal?"

Riley shook her head.

"I ask myself three questions. Does he like kids? Does he like animals? Does he like old people?" She punctuated each question with a stab of her fork. "I'm not talking tolerate here. I'm talking genuinely likes and respects. You find a man that checks all three boxes, and you've found yourself a winner. Our Sam is that guy. Take it from your pal Sara. Sam Walker is a bona fide catch."

"He does seem very kindhearted."

Sara bobbed her head. "Loyal too. He'd never let a buddy down."

"I'll remember that if I'm ever in the market for a man." Riley glanced at the clock before pushing away from the table. "I'm sorry to desert you, but I need to run back to the classroom and eat my energy bar before it's time to take the kids out for recess."

Sara grimaced. "I'm thankful we're not on playground duty this week. It's an oven out there."

Rather than returning the cosmetics bag to her locker, Riley tucked it under her arm as she stood and walked to the door. "When do we get a break from the heat?"

"I forgot you're not a Texas girl. If we're lucky, it'll cool down by Thanksgiving." Sara waved her off with her fork. "*Bon appétit.*"

Riley mulled over Sara's last remark as she walked to her room. She'd also almost forgotten she wasn't a local. Homesickness and grief had taken a back seat to the excitement and busyness of a house full of dogs. Between them and her phone conversations with Sam, suddenly she had happy things to occupy her mind instead of what she'd left behind.

While her class played outside, she dragged one of the two adult-sized chairs she kept in the room to the front. She rechecked her appearance in the small mirror hanging on the back wall before collecting her kids from the playground.

When they returned, Sam stood just outside her door, talking with Mrs. Peeper. He dimpled when he saw her. "Hey, Ms. Vreeland."

Her heart did an odd fluttery thing. "Hi, Officer Sam." Her voice sounded breathless, as though she'd been running on the playground with her students.

He remained by the door, greeting each child with a high five as they entered. When the last one crossed the threshold, he followed.

"So, Ms. Vreeland, are we ready to get started?"

Riley looked up from the note she was making to herself at her desk, and her muscles suddenly clenched with an all-too-familiar tension. Standing in the center of the room, picture book tucked under his arm, was a tall, handsome *cop*. One of the brotherhood. The man she'd come to secretly admire, the friend she'd been eager to see, was eclipsed by the crisp navy uniform he wore.

Heart racing, she forced herself to her feet and stretched a smile on her stiffened lips. "Absolutely." She pointed toward the chair she'd set up for him. "Please have a seat." It was difficult to speak with a dry mouth. "We're excited to hear the story you've chosen for us."

After sitting, he lifted his book to show the cover to the kids. "My story this afternoon is called *Not Today*, and it was written by Lena James."

Riley didn't have to remind the kids to give him their attention. Every wiggling body stilled, and every eye locked on him as he opened the book and began to read.

She was the one having difficulty focusing.

What was the matter with her? What triggered the tension, the dreaded fight-or-flight response that had become second nature to her?

The uniform.

The Sam who came to her rescue after her frantic call wore a T-shirt and jeans. The warm chest she'd dozed on hadn't been shielded with a thick armored vest. The man who'd kept her company as she adjusted to her new dog-mom responsibilities had been a civilian. Even this week, as they'd spoken on the phone, her conversations had been with Sam, not Officer Sam.

The warm feelings she'd developed for him, the fluttering of her heart was for civilian Sam. No way she'd have dropped her guard around a policeman.

In all fairness, in or out of uniform, Sam seemed to be a great guy. Everyone sang his praises.

But he was a cop.

Her only other interaction with a cop had cost her everything. Her home, her sense of security, her life.

She could not afford to forget. Her thoughts spun. She needed to establish some space between them, to put the brakes on her feelings for him. Though she would always be grateful to him as the man who gave her Shadow, they could never be more than friends.

Decision made, her heartbeat slowed, regaining its proper rhythm while she settled in to watch him read to her students. He did it so well. She couldn't imagine Ron—the cop who had made her life a living hell—entertaining a room full of first graders.

Sam and Ron were nothing alike.

And yet . . . Both men were strong, intelligent, take-charge types . . . More importantly, they shared the inescapable bond of their profession.

Why would she put herself at risk again?

"The end." Sam closed the book and placed it in his lap.

Riley stood at her desk. She gave him a brief nod before turning her attention to the class. "Thank you, Officer Sam. Class, wasn't that a great story?"

The kids applauded.

"Everyone take out your crayons and a sheet of paper and draw a picture of your favorite character from the book."

Sam recognized the directions as his cue to leave. While the children were occupied gathering supplies, he walked out into the hall, pausing on the other side of the door to wait for Riley to join him. After a minute or so, it became obvious she wasn't coming.

Careful to stay out of the line of sight of the students, he flagged her over.

She frowned slightly, as if she didn't understand what he was asking. He continued to wave at her until she finally stood and crossed to him. Apparently, she thought he was waiting for a pat on the back. "Thank you for coming. It means so much to the kids."

Had he imagined the formality of her tone or her emphasis on kids? "No problem. Hey, I wondered if you wanted to meet me at Estelle's after school. We could grab a glass of tea and some dessert."

Shaking her head, she took a step toward him and lowered her voice. "No, I don't think so." Hands clasped in front of her, she stared at her shoes. "Look, I'm sorry if I've given you the wrong impression, but I'm not interested in . . . a relationship."

Ouch. He shrugged easily, as though his ego hadn't deflated like a day-old balloon, and forced his lips into a smile. "Did it sound like I was asking you out? My bad. I'm just looking for some company while I eat a piece of Estelle's pie." He waited until she met his eyes. "We're friends, right? It's hard to find someone who's free in the middle of the afternoon, and it's no fun to eat dessert alone."

"I guess I can meet you." Her reluctant acceptance had all the enthusiasm of an inmate on the way to the electric chair and flattened his faltering ego to a latex pancake. "But I can't stay long."

"I'm a pretty fast eater. Why don't you meet me there at four?"

"Okay." She glanced over her shoulder. "I need to get back inside."

"I understand. See you at Estelle's."

Bewildered and a little hurt, he mulled over their exchange as he exited the school. Where was the easy camaraderie they'd shared since the night of Shadow's delivery? What happened to the budding friendship he'd hoped was leading to something more?

He replayed the last few hours, looking for a clue as to what went wrong.

Her smile had been natural enough when their eyes met in the hall. She seemed as happy to see him as he was to see her.

By the time he'd entered the classroom, her expression had cooled considerably. In fact, it looked very much like the wary grimace she'd been passing off as a smile toward him when they first met.

Had he said something, done something, reacted in some way that offended her?

He huffed out a breath of pure frustration.

How could a man raised with two sisters and trained to read body language, facial expressions, and social cues be so clueless when it came to Riley?

And the bigger question, why was he so determined to understand her? This afternoon, she'd made it abundantly clear she was not interested in him. It had taken an embarrassing amount of guilt to coerce her into meeting him after school. Time to let go of both her and any hopes he entertained about a future between them.

Sure, she was pretty. Okay, beautiful. But good looks weren't enough to make him a glutton for punishment. He had *some* self-respect.

He also had a feeling about Riley, not to be confused with his feelings *for* her.

An instructor at the police academy had once told him that intuition was a cop's greatest asset. That truth had resonated with Sam. And because he knew God was the source of all wisdom, he prayed regularly for insight and discernment.

From the first time they met, intuition told him Riley needed something from him, though he doubted she'd ever admit it. His job was to cut through the smoke screens, ferret out the facts, and get to the heart of the problem. He needed to find the answers to help her. And although every previous attempt to get her to open up to him failed, he'd give it another shot over a piece of Estelle's excellent pie.

She walked in the restaurant at straight-up four, looking like she was about to appear before a judge for sentencing. Points for punctuality if not for enthusiasm. He'd been waiting for her beside the ancient cash register at the front of the diner and stepped forward with a smile. "Right on time."

"I wasn't expecting all the cars outside." Somehow she managed to look fresh and lovely in the pretty blue dress that matched her eyes, despite the fact she'd been herding six- and seven-year-olds all day. "I had to park a block away. Estelle's must do quite a business."

"You've never been here?" With a light hand on her shoulder, he directed her around the occupied tables toward an empty booth.

"No, I stick pretty close to home."

He waited until she was seated before sliding onto the vinyl-covered bench across from her. "Why's that? You don't seem the shy, retiring type."

She shrugged as she set her purse on the seat beside her. "I'm cautious."

"And yet you picked up and relocated to a place you'd never been, a place so small it doesn't warrant a dot on the map." He knew he kept harping on the same point, but he sensed everything hinged on that missing piece of the puzzle.

The owner's arrival at their table saved her from giving him an answer.

"Hi, Sam. Who's your friend?" Estelle sent him a look of barely contained curiosity over the top of her half glasses.

"Estelle, I'd like you to meet Riley Vreeland. She's a teacher at County Elementary. Riley, this is Estelle Hill, owner of this fine establishment and maker of the best chocolate pie this side of heaven."

Estelle nodded. "Hey there, Riley. You're staying at the Cooper place, aren't you?"

A flicker of surprise crossed her face. "That's right. I'm renting it for the school year."

"They're good people. I sure hope everything works out for Mrs. Cooper."

Riley smiled. "I'm optimistic. They've got a top team of doctors and a lot of people praying for them."

Estelle pulled a pen and pad from her apron. "What can I get you two?"

He glanced at Riley for confirmation before ordering. "A couple of sweet teas and two slices of chocolate pie, please."

"Coming right up. Glad to meet you, Riley." Estelle gave him a look promising a full inquiry later, then headed off toward the kitchen.

"That was weird." Riley looked more amazed than concerned.

He folded his arms in front of him on the table. "What? The fact that she knows where you live?"

"Yeah. I've never laid eyes on her—"

"Doesn't matter. If you're inside the city limits, you're fair game for the Village Green grapevine."

She glanced around the diner before leaning in to whisper, "I can't be sure, but it appears we're the current buzz on the grapevine."

"You noticed that too? Sorry." He grimaced. "Small-town fact of life. Everyone is up in everybody else's business."

"Does it ever bother you?"

"No, because for the most part, it's harmless." As he looked up, the dozen faces trained on their table quickly swiveled away. "I tell myself they aren't unkind, just nosy."

Her easy laugh sounded more like the Riley he thought he knew. "Very nosy."

Estelle arrived, drinks and dessert on a black plastic tray. She set the food on the table with a conspiratorial wink and left.

Riley watched her departure with a look of misgiving. "I hope people don't get the wrong idea about us."

*Probably wouldn't do any good to tell her it was too late.* "Don't worry. Anybody says anything, I'll set them straight."

He waited, watching as she cut off the end of her pie with the side of her fork and put the delicate bite in her mouth. Her brows shot up. "Oh my gosh. This is amazing."

Satisfied with her response, he picked up his fork. "Told ya."

They ate in companionable silence. First to finish, he pushed away his plate. "So, how'd you like my story today?"

She remained focused on her disappearing slice of pie. "It was cute."

No way he was letting her off with such a nonanswer. "What was your favorite part?"

She lifted her gaze, a faint flush accompanying the guilty look on her face. "I'm sorry. I missed most of it. My mind was wandering. It was about bullying, wasn't it?"

He smiled and nodded. "You heard some of it, anyway. I felt like bullying was a timely message."

A self-conscious look crossed her face so quickly he'd have missed it if he hadn't been watching. She recovered and sent him a smile. "Absolutely. Kids need to be coached on how to handle bullies."

"Kids aren't the only ones. Bullies are everywhere. The trick is to be able to determine when you can handle the situation yourself and when you need to call for backup."

She bent her attention back on her plate. "You make it sound like a job for the police."

He grinned. "Occupational hazard. Although, occasionally, a bullying situation does require police intervention."

"And what if it's the police who are doing the bullying?" She made the offhand comment with a laugh, like she was joking, but the look in her eyes said she was serious. Before he could respond, she changed the subject. "Where do you get the stories you bring to class? The selections you've made so far have been huge hits with the kids."

He played along with the change of topic. *For now.* "The librarian at school should get most of the credit. She gives me a stack of books covering the particular subject I request, then I read through them and choose the one I like best."

She put down her fork to stare at him. "You read stacks of children's books?"

He nodded. "It's a relatively new habit, but yes. It's amazing how the really skilled authors can condense a broad, complex subject to its essence and relate it at its very basic level with a few illustrations and some carefully chosen words. It's been fun to see the looks on the kids' faces as they grasp a concept."

"Now you sound like a teacher."

He shook his head. "I couldn't do it. I love the kids, but there's no way I have the patience to do the stuff you do."

*Oh no.* Out of his peripheral vision he could see Mason and Jane Ryder approaching the table. He'd waved to the older couple when he and Riley had walked past them on their way to the booth and hoped they would be spared a visit.

"We just wanted to stop over and meet your . . . *friend.*" Jane's emphasis on the word suggested all kinds of things.

Her husband rolled his eyes. "Sorry, Sam. I tried to tell her that you and the pretty lady didn't want to be interrupted, but you know how women are."

Sam stood and shook the older man's hand. "No problem. I'm glad you stopped by. Mr. and Mrs. Ryder, I'd like you to meet Riley Vreeland, the new first-grade teacher at County Elementary. The principal has tasked us with finding ways to integrate the friendly presence of law enforcement into the educational system, and we're doing a little brainstorming over some of Estelle's excellent pie."

"It's so nice to meet you, Riley. Mason and I have known Sam all his life. You can imagine we have a particular interest in his girls."

Uh-oh. His dazzling explanation didn't deter her. He didn't dare look at Riley for her reaction, but he knew this wasn't going to go over well. "She's not my girl—"

"Don't let my wife kid you," Mason said. "What she meant to say was she takes a particular interest in everyone's business. There's a word for that . . ."

Jane sent him a quelling look. "I am *not* a busybody. I happen to be a dear friend of Sam's mother, so naturally I'm concerned about the people he's seeing."

"Thank you for your concern, but I'm not *seeing* Ms. Vreeland," Sam said. "Our connection is purely professional."

Mr. Mason tugged at her elbow. "Come on, Jane. Leave the poor kids to their meeting in peace."

"It was so good to meet you, Riley." Jane smiled before turning to pin him with a look. "And Sam, I'll be sure to tell your mother I saw you."

As Mason dragged her away, he could hear her say, "I don't care what he said, that didn't look like any professional meeting I've ever seen."

Riley leaned close. "Do you think anyone in the restaurant missed that conversation?"

He shook his head. "Not a chance. Mason and Jane have only one volume. Loud." He frowned. "I'm sorry."

To his surprise, she laughed. "You handled it beautifully. That bit about finding ways to integrate the friendly presence of police into schools was positively inspired."

Relief that she took it so well brought a smile to his face. "I should have written it down so we can remember it to use the next time."

"Do you think we'll have to explain ourselves again?"

"Oh yeah." He glanced around. "Possibly before we make it out of the restaurant."

Her smile faded. "I should go. I've got papers to grade and puppies to socialize." She picked up her purse and scooted off the bench to her feet.

"How are they doing?" He stood as well.

Her expression softened. "They're starting to open their eyes. It's so cute. Everything I've read says once they open their eyes, it's time for me to begin their interaction with humans, so I'm trying to handle each one several times a day."

He trailed one step behind her as she walked to the front of the diner. "Shadow's okay with that?"

"I think she appreciates the break. If I'm not holding them, they're climbing all over her."

"Poor girl. Hey, if you ever need help with the puppies, I'd be happy to come over and lend a hand." He put the offer out there, partially to test the waters and mostly because he'd like to see her again.

She shut him down with a shake of her head. "No, thanks. I've got it."

He paid the check at the register, despite Riley's protests that she wanted to pay her part. Thankfully, Estelle took the payment without any commentary, though he could tell by the look in her eyes, she'd grill him on the relationship later.

"Thanks for the pie," Riley said as they moved outside into the heat of the afternoon.

"My pleasure. Thanks for keeping me company." He glanced around. "Where'd you park? I'll walk you to your car."

She pointed to her left.

He fell into step beside her. "You know, I feel like you and I have lost some ground."

"What do you mean?" She kept her eyes trained on the sidewalk.

He shrugged. "I dunno. I thought we were good friends, then today at school things felt really awkward."

"I'm sorry." The glance she slanted him was weighted with guilt. "I was preoccupied."

"You want to talk about it?" They stopped beside her vehicle. "I've been told I'm a pretty good listener."

"No. It's nothing." She unlocked and swung open the door of her SUV and climbed in.

"If you change your mind . . ." He closed the door behind her.

After she fired up the engine, she lowered the window. "Really, it's nothing. I need to go. Thanks again."

"No problem." He stepped back and lifted a hand in a wave. "See ya."

That evening, Sam's phone rang a little before seven. "Hey, man."

"Hey yourself, Romeo," Joe said. "I heard you had a hot date with the schoolteacher."

He picked up the television remote and muted the sound. "Who told you that?"

"Who didn't? My cell phone is burning up from all the calls I've had."

"Sounds like a battery issue. And your sources are wrong. Riley kept me company while I had a piece of pie. No big deal."

"Just being neighborly then."

"Exactly."

"And when a young, attractive, single woman decides to hang out with the only eligible bachelor within a twenty-mile radius, people shouldn't read more into it than a simple case of neighborliness."

Time to worry when his friend was being so rational. "Right."

"Even if said couple had, and I quote, 'eyes only for each other,' 'an air of intimacy about them,' and 'they did a lot of whispering'?"

Sam grimaced. "Nobody said that."

"Would your best friend lie to you?"

He snorted derisively. "In a heartbeat."

Joe laughed. "Okay, yeah, I probably would. But I'm being straight with you here. The air waves are buzzing with Village Green's latest romance."

He scrubbed a hand over his face. "Oh man, I'm going to be in so much trouble."

"Why's that?"

"I practically had to force Riley to meet me at Estelle's. Before she agreed, begrudgingly I might add, she told me flat out she's not interested in me."

Joe sucked in a noisy breath. "Dude. That's cold."

*Yeah.* "It's okay. We're just friends. That's why I don't want this stuff to get back to her. She'd freak out."

"There's really nothing there?"

Sam thought about the finality in her voice as she denied his request to hang out with her and the puppies. "Nothing. So if you get any more calls, do me a favor and set them straight."

"Sure thing, bro. You can count on me."

# CHAPTER EIGHT

R iley suffered the familiar sense of fear and self-loathing as she scurried to the garage, dumped her tote and books on the passenger seat, and hurried to climb into the vehicle. As usual, her gaze darted around, searching for signs of Ron.

It had been two months since she packed up and disappeared in the middle of the night. He hadn't found her. Probably wasn't even looking. So why couldn't she just move on?

She hated the power he held over her life, hated the fear-filled recluse she'd become.

Her feelings were exacerbated by the children's book currently occupying her nightstand, the story about bullying Sam had read to her class last week. Something he'd said over chocolate pie that day piqued her interest, and when she got home, she'd ordered a copy online and had it delivered to her door.

She'd read the book through the first time, simply enjoying the colorful illustrations and clever prose the author used to tell the story of barnyard bullying. She'd smiled as she'd turned the pages. Sam had a knack for choosing engaging books.

As she lay in bed that night, the story continued to play through her mind. After the second reading of the book as she ate her dinner the next day, she developed a kinship with the chicken who'd been minding her own business when a goose showed up on the farm, insinuated himself into her life, and proceeded to make her miserable.

The chicken had been gracious at first, extending a warm welcome to the large stranger. It didn't take long for the goose to dominate her, taking advantage of her generosity, and demanding her allotment of feed for himself. When the chicken pushed back, the goose threatened her. Luckily, the farmer noticed her predicament and intervened. He built a strong pen to house the bullying goose, and the chicken's life was restored.

Riley opened the garage door as she started the engine, pulled out as soon as the SUV had adequate clearance, and shut the door again. After checking both sides of the street for suspicious vehicles, she exhaled some of the tension and headed for the school.

When she caught a glimpse of herself in the rearview mirror, she half expected to see the chicken reflected. Her story and the one of the fictional fowl bore many similarities. Like the goose, Ron appeared out of nowhere and immediately began to dominate. Unfortunately, she didn't have a farmer overseer to intervene.

She had God, of course, and continued to pray daily for His help. She believed His promise that he would never leave or forsake her. But honestly, what she really wanted was someone flesh and blood, overalls optional, to come to her defense.

She remembered Sam saying the trick to dealing with bullies was knowing when to handle it yourself, and when to call in backup. From the beginning she'd known she'd needed help. The problem was knowing whom to ask.

Her parents would have been her first option, but they were gone. Her sweet elderly neighbors or any of her friends would have been happy to step in, but realistically, what could they do?

The last thing she wanted was to subject anyone to Ron's wrath. Just thinking of the look in his eyes the night she told him she didn't want to see him anymore sent a cold shiver crawling down her spine. She had no doubt he would hurt anyone who got in his way.

Even now she knew she needed to tell someone. But who?

Sam was the obvious choice. He'd offered a listening ear a dozen times. Kind and compassionate, he was the type of man who lived to help others. He was both willing and able. With the power of law enforcement behind him, he could end this nightmare.

*Or not.*

The reason she hadn't gone to the police in Oklahoma was the same reason she couldn't talk to Sam. He was a cop. If Ron had not already joined the force in Oklahoma, he would soon. It was only a matter of time. And the brotherhood would side against her.

Her case against Ron was weak. Other than the night when he'd grabbed her, he'd never done anything overtly threatening that she could accuse him of. She could say he'd stalked her. But then he would say their meetings were coincidental. Her word against his. And because he was law enforcement, they would side with him and dismiss her fears and suspicions as emotional fallout from the grief of losing her parents.

Somehow Ron would find out she'd talked to the police—they were his friends after all—and then she'd be in real danger with nowhere to turn.

She pulled into the school parking lot and took a deep breath. Time to work. Riley picked up a heavy cardboard stop sign from the box in the administrative closet and walked out the front entrance of the school. Sara met her at the crosswalk, a cup of coffee in one hand and stop sign in the other.

Riley saluted her with the paddle. "Good morning. What's your pleasure, cars or buses?"

"I don't know about pleasure," Sara groused. "I guess I'll take buses this morning. The walk will do me good."

"Deal. I'll trade with you this afternoon if you like."

"We can decide over lunch. I can't make these difficult decisions until after I've had my infusion of caffeine."

Riley laughed, watching her friend walk to the cafeteria entrance where the buses loaded and unloaded.

Parking lot duty rotated through the staff, like lunchroom and playground responsibilities. Working the parking lot was Riley's least favorite assignment, probably because she felt so exposed. On the plus side, it gave her the opportunity to be outdoors. The mid-October mornings had begun to cool off with the promise of sweater days in the near future.

A fragrant fall breeze stirred her hair and carried a wave of homesickness. Autumn was always a busy time in a household of educators, but she and her parents had delighted in slowing down to watch the seasons change.

She still missed them every day. She missed the house they'd lived in for nearly fifty years, filled with reminders of the love they shared. When she'd pulled out of the driveway in the middle of the night, headlights off to escape notice, she'd vowed she'd return and take back the life and memories Ron had stolen from her.

Unlike her chicken counterpart, she was making very little progress.

A silver minivan pulled up in front of the school and stopped. The side doors slid open, and five kids sprang out onto the sidewalk.

"Good morning." Riley greeted the children and waved to the driver as she pulled away from the curb.

Traffic increased. Vehicles pulled up, disgorged their passengers, and eased away in a seamless progression. She welcomed each of the students, delighted she could call many by name.

Closer to eight, the steady stream slowed to a trickle. An older Honda Accord stopped at the curb less than five feet from where

Riley stood at the painted crosswalk. It sounded like the radio was blaring, but when she looked through the windshield, she could see the couple in front—Chris Enslow's mom and a man Riley didn't recognize—arguing. Shouting.

Chris climbed out of the back seat, dragging his backpack, and said something to the man before slamming the door.

Face contorted with rage, the man bolted from the car and snatched Chris by the collar, shaking him like a ragdoll. "Don't you ever mouth off to me like that, you little snot."

Feet dangling several inches from the ground, Chris shot back, "You can't talk to my mom like that."

Riley and Mrs. Enslow arrived at his side at the same time.

"Put him down!" both women demanded in unison.

"Mind your own business," he snarled at Riley.

Mrs. Enslow sucked in a shocked breath. "Don't talk to her that way. That's Chris's teacher."

He shoved Chris aside, the child dropping to the ground in a boneless heap, and grabbed Chris's mother roughly by the arm. "I'll talk to her any way I please."

Fury pushed Riley past her fears. "Let go of her right now, you bully!"

Eyes lit with pure evil glared into hers. "Lady, I warned you once. Do you have any idea what happens to people who get in my way?"

Chris's mom struggled in his grasp. "Leave her alone, Hector."

"Shut up." He swung and slapped her, the sound ringing out. He pushed her away.

Riley was only vaguely aware of Chris bending over his mother, as her attention was pinned on the menacing expression of the man towering over her. She swallowed hard. He was going to tear her limb from limb.

"I told you to mind your own business." He clamped his hand over her upper arm and yanked.

As he dragged her closer, Riley reared back and bashed him on the head with her stop sign. "They *are* my business."

She didn't know who was more shocked, her or Hector. He froze long enough for her to wind up for another blow.

Someone ran up behind her. "Ms. Vreeland, why don't you let me take it from here?" *Sam!* Relief flooded through her. No voice had ever sounded sweeter.

He muscled his way between the combatants. "Sir, you'll want to release the lady's arm. Now!"

Riley lowered her sign. Hector dropped his hand and took a step backward. "She hit me. Did you see it? She hit me."

"Sir, I not only saw it, I filmed it with my cop cam." He grinned. "That footage is going to make you a star."

Sam glanced toward the school entrance. "Ah, Mrs. Peeper. Perfect timing. Would you escort the Enslows and Ms. Vreeland into the building?" He turned to the crowd gathered around them. "That's all folks. Show's over. Parents, let's get these kids into school."

"Mrs. Enslow, let's have the nurse look at your cheek, shall we?" Mrs. Peeper calmly rounded up her charges and, with an arm behind each woman, directed them inside. "Chris, while I take care of your mother, would you stop in at the counselor's office? You've had a rough morning. I think it would be a good idea for you to talk to her about it."

He hugged his mom, shot a wide smile at Riley, and skipped down the hall toward the counselor.

Mrs. Peeper watched his progress down the hall. "Aren't children wonderfully resilient?" She turned to Riley. "Ms. Vreeland, will you wait for me in my office while I walk Mrs. Enslow to the nurse? I won't be but a moment."

"Yes, ma'am."

Mrs. Enslow caught Riley's hand before she could leave. "Thank you for taking up for me and Chris. Not many people would do what you did. You're a very brave woman."

Riley didn't feel very brave as she made her way to the administration offices on wobbly legs. The rush of adrenaline spent, she was left with the jittery aftermath and the real fear she'd just lost her job. Maybe her vocation. She didn't think violence would look too good in her teaching file.

Miserable, she ducked her head as she hurried past the secretary and into Mrs. Peeper's office. Unable to sit, she pushed the door closed and paced the short space in front of the principal's desk.

She didn't have long to wait. As soon as her boss shut the door, Riley stopped pacing to face her. "I'm so sorry, Mrs. Peeper. I never intended—"

Face grim, the principal lifted her hand for silence, and Riley's heart sank. "You never have to apologize to me for protecting a student. I'm the one who's sorry you were exposed to such a frightening experience. I'll be happy to send a substitute to your room and drive you home for the day."

Riley couldn't believe her ears. "You're not mad I conked him on the head?"

"Are you kidding? I'm only sorry the signs aren't heavier and that you didn't get to hit him again."

After a stunned beat, both women burst into wild laughter.

"He looked so surprised," Riley managed between guffaws.

Mrs. Peeper dabbed at tears in her eyes. "He probably didn't expect that much fight from a woman."

When the laughter finally died down, Riley asked, "Who *was* he?"

Her boss shrugged. "I have no idea. Sam can fill us in on all the details. In the meantime, let me find someone to take your class, and I'll take you home for a well-earned day off."

"If it's okay with you, I'll stay. I'm not traumatized. If anything, I'm pumped from all that adrenaline. The whole thing will probably blow over faster if we just go on as usual."

Mrs. Peeper studied her face. "You're sure?"

Riley nodded. "Yes, ma'am."

"I like your style, Ms. Vreeland." She grinned as she waved her off. "Well, get on with you. The tardy bell will ring in two minutes."

Sam arrived in the administrative offices a little past one. "Hey, Ms. Schmidt. Is Mrs. Peeper around?"

"Yes, and she told me to send you in as soon as you arrived."

"Thanks." He walked the short corridor, knocked on the principal's door, and let himself in.

Mrs. Peeper smiled. "Thank you for coming. That was quite a bit of excitement on my front lawn this morning."

"Yes, ma'am." He wasn't ready to smile about it yet. Probably never would. He'd never recover from seeing the murderous look in Hector's eyes as he'd wrapped a beefy hand around Riley's arm. If anything had happened to her . . .

Mrs. Peeper reached for the phone on her desk. "Let me ask Ms. Vreeland to join us for the briefing. She'll be interested in the details, and this way you'll only have to repeat them once."

"Good idea."

After calling down to the first-grade classroom, she lowered the receiver into the cradle. "How in the world did you get here so quickly this morning? It was mostly over before I was even aware there was a situation."

"Sara was on bus duty and heard the shouting. She called 9-1-1. I was just two blocks away when the dispatch came in, so it didn't take me any time to get here." Thank God. If he'd have been even a minute later . . .

"I'm grateful for your quick intervention. Our Ms. Vreeland is a plucky little thing, but I am all too aware things could have gone badly."

There was a tap on the door, and Riley pushed it open and stepped into the office. She smiled at the principal, then turned to greet him. "Hey, Sam. Excellent timing this morning."

Her cavalier attitude was the last straw. "Really. That's all you have to say?"

"Come on, Sam," Mrs. Peeper protested. "Riley's a hero. She got a standing ovation in the cafeteria."

"She could have been killed." He refused to share in their good humor.

Riley sniffed as though her feelings were injured, clearly not grasping the severity of the situation. "Oh, well."

"Would you like to know about the man you were wrestling on the lawn this morning?"

She lifted her chin. Another sniff. "We were hardly wrestling—"

"Hector Bova is a repeat felon. Assault is his crime of choice." He paused, waiting until Riley's gaze met his. "He enjoys beating people to a pulp."

The indulgent smile disappeared from the principal's face. "I hope you arrested him."

"I did. And I'll make sure he gets sent away for a long time."

Riley's brow furrowed. "What was a felon doing with Mrs. Enslow?"

"He was her roommate." He released a long breath. "You both know Darcie—Mrs. Enslow—was having financial trouble. When I did a welfare check, she told me she'd been out of work for a couple weeks and bills had piled up. She'd found another job by then, waitressing in a restaurant in Corsicana, but her weeks of unemployment had eaten up her cash reserves. She talked about getting a roommate to help with expenses. I asked her to let me interview prospective candidates, but she met this guy, Bova, at work and he seemed 'nice,' so she invited him to live with her and Chris."

"What was a felon doing working at a restaurant?"

"He's on parole, employed as a dishwasher."

"And living with Chris and his mother." Riley clapped a hand over her heart as the implications finally dawned on her. "He could have killed them."

"I'm glad to see you're taking it seriously."

She turned her blue-green gaze on him, her expression contrite. "I'm sorry if I frightened you."

"*Frightened* me?" Was she kidding? He studied her face, her eyes, and found only well-meaning sincerity. She really didn't get it. "Riley, you shaved ten years off my life. When I saw the look on his face, I swear I saw *your* life flash before *my* eyes."

Mrs. Peeper glanced at her silent cell phone then stood. "I'm sorry. I need to answer this. Will you excuse me for a moment?"

She walked to the door. "This should take five minutes. Don't anybody leave until I get back."

He waited until the latch clicked behind her before turning back to Riley. "You okay? Really?"

Gaze locked with his, she nodded. "I wasn't hurt. Just scared. I was so happy to see you."

He pushed to his feet. "Stand up."

"Okay." Slowly she stood and faced him. "Why?"

"Because I need a hug."

Her brows shot up. "Is this some little-known police procedure?"

Grinning, he shook his head. "Strictly personal. And don't worry. You don't have to hug me back. This is not about romance. I just need some solid reassurance that you're okay after you scared me to death."

To his surprise, she walked willingly into his arms. "I was only going to point out Mrs. Peeper will be back any minute."

"She said five. I only need two." He pulled her to his chest, resting his cheek on top of her head. Her hair was silky against his skin. He inhaled deeply. "Mmmm. You smell really nice. Okay, maybe three."

She giggled as he held her close.

The steady rhythm of her heart against his was a comforting antidote to the fears that continued to play through his mind. Bova hadn't hurt her. She was okay. "Riley, what were you thinking this morning?"

After several beats of silence, she sighed heavily. "I didn't want to be the chicken anymore."

Hands still on her shoulders, he pulled back to look her in the eyes. "Honey, you're not a chicken."

"Not *a* chicken. *The* chicken."

"Uh, okay. Sure." He checked her pupils, looking for signs of shock. "I'm wondering if this is some kind of PTSD reaction." He was only half kidding.

She shook her head. "I'm talking about the chicken in the book you read to my class last week. You know, the one about bullying."

He thought back to what felt like a lifetime ago, searching his mind for the details of story time. "The goose was picking on the chicken, right?"

Riley nodded. "Exactly. She didn't stand up for herself when he bullied her. She backed off and let him take everything."

His grip on her shoulders tightened slightly as he frowned into her face. "The point of the story was that the bully was too strong for her to handle alone. She needed to ask for help."

"True, but everything happened so fast this morning, there was no time to ask for help." She smiled. "Doesn't matter. You showed up and vanquished the bully."

But what if he'd been five minutes later? He drew her against him again, once more, just to reassure himself she was safe. "Lesson learned. No more books with drama. From now on we're sticking with *See Spot Run*."

She was still in his arms, laughing, when Mrs. Peeper reentered the office. The principal acknowledged the embrace with a brisk nod of her head. "Good. Looks like you two have worked things out."

They split apart with guilty haste.

Sam cleared his throat. "It's not what it looks like."

"We're just friends," Riley added.

Mrs. Peeper's expression remained neutral as she moved behind her desk. "Thank you for clearing that up. Now if both of you will take a seat, I'd like to run something by you before Ms. Vreeland goes back to class." She looked at him. "That is, assuming you have nothing to add on this morning's altercation."

He shook his head. "The school's clear. Darcie will have to appear in court when it comes to trial, but I think we can keep Riley out of it. I'll take a statement to have on file, just in case."

"Good." The principal settled into her chair and folded her hands on the desk. "If you'll indulge me, I'd like to switch gears for a moment and talk about the Fall Festival on the Green. Riley, as a new resident, you probably aren't familiar with the tradition, but every year the town puts on a fall carnival for the kids as an alternative to trick-or-treating. Each business and organization is responsible for providing a booth. It can be a game, or an activity, or just a place to pick up goodies. For the past couple years, County Elementary has partnered with the police department to sponsor a booth. If you're willing, I'd like you and Sam to take the lead this year."

Riley nodded. "Sure. No problem."

The older woman beamed. "Thank you. You have such a gift for creativity. I know you'll come up with something wonderful."

"I'll try." After a moment of weighted silence, Riley looked from Mrs. Peeper to Sam and back to the principal. "If that's everything, I'd better get back to my class."

"Officer Sam, do you have any further questions for Ms. Vreeland?"

He shook his head.

"Then we're good." She nodded her dismissal to Riley. "Thanks for coming."

Sam stood as Riley left. When the door closed behind her, he directed a pointed look at the principal. "That was a short five minutes."

She had the grace to look embarrassed. "I'm so sorry, Sam. I could see the two of you needed a moment, so I thought I'd just step out. Once I got into the hall, I realized I couldn't leave the administrative offices without getting caught by someone needing something, so I had to stay close. I didn't want to hover by the door like an eavesdropper, so I ended up lurking by Mrs. Schmidt's desk and making her nervous. When she asked me for the third time if something was wrong, I knew I had to come back. I'm sorry I interrupted—"

He lifted his palms. "It was nothing. Really. We're just friends."

"Of course." Eyes down, she busied herself with the papers on her desk. "Sometimes friends just need a hug."

"Exactly."

"She's a wonderful girl, our Ms. Vreeland." By now she'd squared off all the piles and moved on to corralling pens. "Beautiful, smart, compassionate, brave . . . single."

"She's a friend."

Mrs. Peeper lifted her gaze to his. "So you've said. Repeatedly."

"Having a hard time making people believe me."

She coughed into her hand. "I can't imagine why. It's probably because of all the romance in the air. First Trey and Hallie, then Joe and Eden . . ."

He narrowed his eyes at her. "More likely because Village Green is populated with the biggest busybodies on the planet."

She grinned. "So true." She pulled a printed sheet of paper from the stack in front of her and slid it across the desk. "Here's the information on the organizational meeting Friday night for the Fall Festival. Would you mind sharing it with Riley?"

He spared a brief glance at the paper before spearing her with a suspicious scowl. "This isn't some kind of misbegotten attempt at matchmaking, is it?"

She straightened. "What do you mean?"

He held up the page. "It looks to me like you're trying to throw Riley and me together."

"Heavens no!" Her affronted expression appeared genuine. "Riley is so clever and talented, the best County Elementary has to offer. And I know Officer Bob has represented the police at the booth for the last couple of years, but he's such a grouch. You have a wonderful rapport with the kids already, which makes you the perfect choice for the position."

She paused to send him a scolding frown. "Obviously it's been a crazy day, otherwise you wouldn't be accusing your friend and former principal of such base dealings."

It was his turn to look embarrassed. "I'm sorry. It has been crazy." He stood. "If that's all, I need to get back to the station."

"That's it. Thank you for coming."

He had his hand on the doorknob when she added, "And thank you for taking such good care of us, Sam."

# CHAPTER NINE

Friday night, Sam felt something akin to panic. "It's not too late. You can still turn back."

"Would you stop saying that?" Riley gave him a shove. "I'm not going anywhere. Mrs. Peeper assigned us to the Fall Festival, and I'm going to do my part."

He repositioned himself at her side, shoulders almost touching as they walked swiftly through the early evening shadows. Even though he agreed to pick her up, he remained unconvinced she should attend the meeting. "But there's no reason for both of us to go. I promise I'll take good notes and relay the details to you. You can go home and work on lesson plans or something."

She paused long enough to send him a frown. "I don't do lesson plans on Friday night. And why are you trying to get rid of me? Are you embarrassed to be seen with me?"

"Are you kidding?" What man in his right mind wouldn't be proud to have this beautiful woman at his side? This beautiful *friend*. He lowered his voice though they were the only ones on the sidewalk. "If you want the truth, I'm embarrassed about the people you're going to meet."

She rolled her eyes. "That's silly. Everyone I've met in Village Green seems very nice."

He snorted. "Very nosy, you mean. You can't have forgotten our trip to Estelle's?"

She dismissed the reminder with a wave of her hand. "We were a novelty, but you explained we were there on official business, and now everybody knows. It should be obvious to the people present at the meeting that we're there to work on the festival. End of discussion."

"You'd think so, but this *is* Village Green," he muttered.

"Stop worrying. We'll keep a low profile, and everything will be fine."

"Hold that thought."

The bell on the door of Estelle's jingled when he pulled it open and stepped aside for Riley to enter ahead of him.

"Hi, y'all. Glad you could make it." Estelle smiled broadly. "I think Trey saved you a place at his table."

"Thanks." Hand at her back, Sam directed Riley through the noisy, crowded room to a round table for six, uncomfortably situated dead center of the diner. His friends and their wives were already seated.

Trey and Joe stood as they arrived.

"Hey, man." Trey shook Sam's hand, then Riley's. "Hi, I'm Trey Gunther." He pointed to the woman next to him. "And this is my wife, Hallie."

Riley smiled and nodded. "Hi Trey, Hallie. I'm Riley Vreeland."

Joe slapped him on the back and greeted Riley before pointing to the vacant spots next to Eden at the table. "The mayor's about to start. Have a seat."

Sam pulled out the chair for Riley and waited until she settled in before taking the seat beside her. He made a quick scan of the restaurant, telling himself the increased buzz had nothing to do with their arrival.

Mayor Sellers walked to the makeshift podium, a cardboard box set on a table beside the cash register, and tapped the mic twice. "Good evening. Let's get started so we can get out of here and on to the football game. I've got a good feeling our boys are going to carry us to State this year."

Everyone cheered.

"Let me begin by saying thank you to Estelle for closing early tonight so we could have our meeting. She wants me to tell you she's got a table set up in the back with water and tea, should anybody get thirsty." The mayor's gaze searched the crowd before coming to rest on Sam. "Before we open this up to Fall Festival business, I feel it's only right to recognize Village Green's very own crime fighting duo. Sam, you and your lady friend stand up so everyone can see you."

*So much for keeping a low profile.* After a brief hesitation, he got to his feet, Riley following his lead. He shot her a look of apology.

His face heated as the room erupted in applause. After what felt like the longest minute of Sam's life, Mayor Sellers signaled for silence. "For any of you who've been living under a rock these last few days and missed the excitement, let me catch you up-to-date. At the elementary school on Monday of this week, a paroled felon took a swing at one of our students and his mother. Quick-thinking Miss Vreeland smashed him over the head with her crossing guard stop sign, subduing him long enough for Sam to arrive and cuff him."

Over the sound of renewed clapping, Sam could clearly hear the remarks from the old men seated at the table beside theirs.

"Pretty little thing can't weigh more than a hundred pounds soaking wet. She doesn't look strong enough to subdue a bunny rabbit, much less a felon."

"Maybe she knows karate."

Hands lifted for quiet, the mayor addressed Sam and Riley. "I know I speak for all of us when I say good work you two and thank you for keeping our children safe."

More enthusiastic applause. Sam acknowledged it with a dip of his chin and sat. Though he didn't turn around, he could see from the corner of his eye that Riley did the same.

"Now, on to our main topic of business—our Fall Festival at the end of the month. As you know, we decided to consolidate citywide trick-or-treating to one event on the green. It makes a nice community gathering, and it's easier for parents to keep up with their kiddies." The mayor lifted a sheet of paper. "I have a list here of the activities we've provided in the past and the groups who sponsored them. I'll read through it, and you all let me know if you're planning to do the same thing again this year."

"You think Sam and the lady are sweethearts?" The semi-whispered remark from Eddie Bray, one of the old guys at their right, seemed to echo in the room.

"I don't know," Chet said, "but I always say, where there's smoke, there's fire."

"I don't smell any smoke." Eddie sniffed deeply. "You're probably just smelling grease from the kitchen."

"It's a figure of speech."

"Need I remind you I only went through the tenth grade? We didn't learn no figures of speech. I'd appreciate it if you'd talk plain and leave the speech figures to the college kids."

Sam's buddies were certainly enjoying this. Joe coughed into his fist to cover his laugh. Trey ducked his head and snickered.

"Eddie and Chet, you fellas need to keep it down back there so folks can hear what I'm reading."

"Sorry, Mayor. I was just asking Chet whether Sam and the lady—"

Sam shot to his feet and practically shouted, "The police department and County Elementary plan to sponsor the dart-throwing booth like we did last year."

He caught Riley's look of surprise and sent her an almost imperceptible shrug of apology.

Mayor Sellers nodded. "Thanks, Sam. Appreciate you getting the ball rolling. I'm marking you down. Now what about the Grocery Giant? Do you folks want to do the ring toss again this year?"

"Nice distraction, officer," Joe whispered. "You may actually get out of here alive."

*Not likely.* Sam slunk down in his chair. "Riley's going to kill me."

"Maybe she didn't hear."

"Are you kidding? I'm sure they heard Chet and Eddie down at the station."

His best friend's shoulders bounced with suppressed laughter. "You're right. She's going to kill you."

In his defense, he'd warned her. Multiple times. He'd known the sight of the two of them together would incite talk. Unfortunately, forewarning didn't make the reality any less awful. After tonight, the whole town would think they were an item, which would be funny except that they weren't, and he wished they were. Folks would rib him about his relationship with Riley, then he'd be forced to deny it, which would convince them he was hiding something.

Where there's smoke, there's fire.

Then one day, Riley would move on from Village Green or worse, find someone here she *was* interested in, and he'd be left standing, alone. The last of the three musketeers.

First to fall was Trey, who reconnected with his high-school sweetheart.

Confirmed bachelor, Joe, followed close behind him, falling hard for Eden and her son when they rolled into town.

Both men found their match with women whose personalities and histories meshed perfectly with their own. And though it was a bit nauseating to watch them in all their newlywed bliss, he was genuinely happy for them.

He'd known the day would come when the threesome would go their separate ways to start families of their own. He'd just never imagined he'd be left behind.

The only one who couldn't get a girl.

In the previous week, he'd deflected at least a half dozen remarks from well-meaning people asking him when it was his turn. He'd laughed them off, touting the blessedness of being single, but deep down, he was wondering the same thing. When was it his turn?

His sister had been offering to fix him up with friends for years, and he'd always refused. It was bad enough he couldn't find someone on his own. To rely on his sister fell into the realm of pathetic.

Recently, he'd filled out an application for one of those online dating services but hadn't pushed *send*.

What was he waiting for?

God.

Sam had always believed He would bring the right woman when the time was right. When Riley showed up in town and he got to know her better, he'd begun to think, to hope, she was the one. Wrong.

Was his faith too simplistic? Was it naive to believe the Almighty was in the matchmaking business?

Beside him, Joe stood, dragging Sam back from his ruminations. "Paradise Bakery would like to sponsor a booth this year. We'll offer a cupcake walk."

The mayor nodded. "Thank you, Joe and Eden. That's very generous of you. I don't know what a cupcake walk is, but if it involves goodies from your bakery, I'll be the first in line."

The group laughed.

"I'm looking at my list," he continued, "and it appears we've covered all the previous participants and added some new ones. I appreciate you folks, and I'm certain our kids will have a special night. Oh wait, there is one more thing." The mayor scanned the crowd, his gaze coming to rest on their table.

"Hallie, are you willing to handle the media aspect of the festival?"

She nodded. "Yes, sir, I'm on it. I've already posted the early details on the city website. I'll continue to update it with information and pictures as I get them."

"Thank you so much. I don't know what we'd do without you."

Trey added a rousing amen.

When the laughter died down, Mayor Sellers said, "Thank you all for coming out and putting in a good night's work. Pastor Dale, why don't you come up here and close us in prayer so we can get over to the stadium and cheer on our boys? And folks, remember as you're leaving to carry your glasses to the counter and throw away your trash, so Estelle isn't here all night cleaning up after us."

After the meeting dismissed, the six of them remained seated as the others filed past.

"You going to the game?" Trey asked.

Sam shook his head. "We're heading back to Riley's place."

"Why don't you and Hallie join us?" Riley said. "The vet told me I need to socialize the puppies, and Sam agreed to help. The more people the puppies meet, the better."

"I bet they're getting big." Eden had to lean in to be heard over the noise of the departing crowd.

Riley nodded. "They'll be three weeks old tomorrow. They're already trying to climb out of the pool. If you've got time, I'd love for you and Joe to come over tonight and see them."

Eden glanced at Joe, who nodded. "Sure. That'd be great."

After agreeing to meet at Riley's, the three couples stood and joined the thinning crowd moving toward the door.

Pastor Dale caught up with Sam, placing a hand on his shoulder and said in a low voice, "I wanted you to know I got in touch with Darcie, and she and I are going to meet tomorrow."

"Thank you for following up on that."

The older man nodded. "I'm happy to do it." He looked past Sam to Riley who followed directly behind him. "Are you going to introduce me to your intrepid friend?"

Sam moved aside for Riley to stand next to him. "Pastor Dale, I want you to meet Riley Vreeland, the newest addition to the staff at County Elementary."

Dale took her outstretched hand. "It's a pleasure to meet you, Riley. Am I correct in assuming you've taken Mrs. Cooper's place as first-grade teacher?"

"Yes, sir."

"I know they're happy to have you." His eyes danced. "I'm sure you had no idea you'd be thwarting villains when you took the job."

She laughed. "My part in the situation has been grossly exaggerated. Give it another week in the gossip mill, and I'll have single-handedly subdued him with my ninja skills. Truthfully, it was Sam who handled it. I was more of a grateful bystander."

Pastor Dale nodded as he turned his gaze toward Sam. "We are very blessed to have Sam to protect us. He's a good man to have around."

Riley smiled over at Sam, handsome in his polo and jeans. "He certainly is."

She'd missed him. After she told him she wasn't looking for a romantic relationship, he hadn't contacted her. They hadn't spoken until Monday when he rescued her at the school. She'd told herself it was okay, that she needed to maintain a distance from him, but she'd missed him. A lot. She'd been looking for an excuse to reconnect with him when Mrs. Peeper assigned them the same booth at the Fall Festival.

"He's rescued me so often, I owe him big-time."

The pastor shook his head. "Sam's not the kind to keep score."

Probably not. She studied him from the corner of her eye. Solid and dependable. Sam appeared to be the rare type driven by some inner nobility of character, a goodness that went to his marrow.

Still, she didn't want to be on the receiving end all the time. Which was why she invited his friends over this evening. It was her turn to rescue him.

She'd caught the sly looks passing between them—the ones that said they thought she and Sam were a couple. Sam had expressed his embarrassment that nothing he said would dissuade them or the town from thinking he and Riley were an item. Maybe she could help.

Pastor Dale turned his warm but penetrating gaze on her. "Has anyone invited you to church yet?"

"Yes, sir. Sam, Mary Jo Piermont, and several of the teachers from school have all extended invitations."

He smiled with obvious approval. "Good. I'd hate to think we were dropping the ball." He lifted a bushy brow. "So why haven't I seen you there?"

Sam shifted slightly, angling his shoulder in front of hers as though to deflect any criticism. "She hasn't been in Village Green that long. It takes a while to settle in—"

The older man chuckled. "Whoa there, officer. You don't have to protect her from me. I was just curious." He turned to Riley.

"You'll forgive the frank speech of an old man, I hope? At my age, I can't afford to waste time dillydallying."

She smiled at his use of the old-fashioned phrase. "I appreciate the honesty. And I've been planning to come." *Once I get past this fear of Ron finding me.* "I guess I've been . . . dillydallying."

"It happens to the best of us." He rubbed his chin in a considering way. "This Sunday would be an excellent week to join us. I'm starting a new sermon series on Hebrews." He nodded toward Sam. "If he's not on duty, get this fella here to bring you. It's always easier to go someplace new with a friend."

She darted a glance at Sam. "Thank you. We'll see."

"I guess I'd best get to work. I told Estelle I'd help her load the dishwasher so she can get on to the game." He took several steps toward the kitchen before turning to call over his shoulder, "Good night, y'all. Happy to meet you, Riley."

She waved. "Nice to meet you, Pastor Dale. See you Sunday."

Sam waited until they were seated in the privacy of his truck to bring up the subject of church attendance. "You don't have to go, you know."

Riley shook her head. "It's time. I've missed being in church. Listening to podcasts of my preacher back home is not the same."

He started the engine and eased onto the street. "I'm off on Sunday if you want to go with me."

Her laugh came out as a snort. "No way. I heard the whispers and saw the looks we were getting tonight. If I showed up beside you in church, they'd be announcing our engagement by the closing hymn."

He looked away from the road momentarily to meet her eyes. "I'm really sorry. I told you we'd keep a low profile and then the mayor stands us up in front of everybody. It just went downhill from there. I knew it would be bad, but I didn't see that coming."

"You don't need to apologize. You tried to warn me, and I wouldn't listen. It's a testimony to your good nature that you haven't said I told you so, like I deserve."

"You deserve to live your life in peace, without a bunch of interfering busybodies." He sounded really upset. "I'm guessing now that you've had a real taste of small-town life, you're wishing you never landed in our little burg."

She sent him a smile. "Wrong. I still think Village Green is a great place."

Her answer seemed to ease some of the tension in his posture. "I'm glad. You've never told me why you decided to move here."

Actually, she'd told him half a dozen times. He just wasn't satisfied with her answer. "I was in the dentist's office—"

He took a right off Main and guided the truck along her street. "Yeah, I've got the part about the article in the travel magazine prompting you to relocate. What I don't get is the why. Why would you give up your job and home and friends—"

Her house came into view. To forestall the conversation she wasn't ready to have, she pointed to the vehicles parked in front. "Oh, look. Everybody's already here."

"It was nice of you to invite them."

"Nice nothing. It was strategy. If the people closest to you think something's going on between us, everyone else will too."

He pulled into the driveway and shut off the engine. "I've told them we're just friends."

"I know you have." She smiled at the look of pure frustration in his eyes. "Old friends are the hardest people to get through to because they think they know us better than we know ourselves. I'm hoping when they spend some time with us, they'll realize nothing's going on. Once they get the message, they can spread it for us. That'll get the matchmakers off our backs."

He circled in front of the truck and opened her door. "If you say so."

The two couples waited for them in the rocking chairs on the front porch.

"What took you so long?" Joe asked. "Did you stop to sign autographs?"

The others laughed.

"No, just a grilling from Pastor Dale, and we were on our way."

Frowning, Trey laid a hand on Sam's shoulder. "Aw, man, that had to be the clincher on a night of embarrassment. I'm sorry." He turned to Riley. "I might as well give it to you straight. You're one of us now, so everybody will feel entitled to be up in your business."

His wife nodded. "I affectionately refer to it as living life in a fishbowl. I'm not sure you'll ever enjoy it, but I promise eventually you'll get used to it."

"It's okay." Riley unlocked the front door, switched on the light in the hall and motioned for everyone to enter. "It's nice to know somebody cares. I don't have any family to meddle."

Eden stepped inside, Joe right behind her. "Mary Jo mentioned your parents had died. Do you have any siblings?"

Riley shook her head. "It's just me."

Joe dipped his head toward his wife. "Don't tell Eden or she'll be trying to adopt you." He wrapped an arm around Eden. "My girl here is all about family."

"It's true." Eden's beautiful face was filled with compassion. "And you're welcome to join ours."

Riley felt the warmth of offered friendship right down to her toes. "Thank you."

She'd second-guessed her decision to move to Village Green since she got here. Almost daily she asked herself whether she should have stayed in Oklahoma City and found a way to dislodge

Ron. And if a move was inevitable, should she have chosen a metropolitan area with more opportunities? But even as she debated her choices, she couldn't deny she'd met some truly wonderful people here.

Shadow strolled into the entrance hall, wagging her tail in enthusiastic greeting.

Riley crouched, circling the dog with her arms, and looked up at Hallie and Trey. "Let me introduce you to my four-legged family. This is Shadow, woman's best friend and mother to four adorable puppies."

After everyone gave the dog a pat or scratch on the back, Riley waved them toward the hall. "This way to the nursery."

She flipped on the overhead light in the guest bedroom and the puppies sprang to life. Yipping with delight, they scrambled to the edge of the plastic pool on wobbly legs, trying desperately to escape and join the party.

Sam hung back at the door with her to watch them. "They're going to be out of there any day now. You know that, right?"

Riley grimaced. "I know. Mr. Buchanan has ordered me a crate for them. I just hope it's here before they crack the code."

Hallie crouched on her knees, poolside. She turned an imploring look at Riley. "Can I hold one?"

"Absolutely. Everyone who wants to, help yourself."

Trey scooped one up and, holding the squirming puppy to his chest, faced Riley. "There's got to be a story here. How did you end up with a house full of dogs?"

"I blame my buddy Sam entirely." She cocked a thumb in Sam's direction.

Trey frowned at him in confusion. "You brought her a dog with puppies?"

"He brought me a dog with fleas," Riley corrected. "We didn't discover she was pregnant until later."

Trey's brows shot up. "Smooth move, officer. Nice way to ingratiate yourself with the lady."

Sam shrugged, taking the teasing in stride. "Poor dog needed a home. I figured a woman who could handle a room full of six- and seven-year-olds would be just the person to rescue her."

"I wasn't too thrilled when he arrived with her." She smiled at Sam. "Do you remember how badly she stank?"

A dimple appeared in his cheek, and his eyes lit. "I remember how mad you were when I washed her in your fancy shampoo."

Riley turned from him to direct her remarks to the others. "He walks into my house, bedraggled animal in his arms, and starts ordering me around. Before I knew it, he'd plunked her down in my sparkling clean bathtub and was scrubbing her with my expensive shampoo."

"That sounds like Sam, all right." Joe said. "He can't help taking charge. He's been bossing us around since we were kids."

As Sam nodded his acknowledgement of an obviously oft-repeated accusation, Riley felt the strangest urge to defend him, an urge that confused her. When had his bossiness, a trait that regularly set her teeth on edge, suddenly become an admirable quality?

She rested a hand on Sam's forearm and flashed him a smile of support. "He's got good instincts. And while I would never have asked for a dog, Shadow's been such a blessing to me. Honestly, I'm not sure who rescued who."

Eden sat cross-legged on the floor next to Hallie and peered over the edge of the pool at the primarily black puppies, each with a random patch or two of white fur. "They are so cute. How do you tell them apart since they look so much alike?"

"She color coded them." Sam pointed to the puppies wrestling in their blue plastic corral. "See how each one has a different colored collar?"

"I'm calling them Red, Blue, Green, and Pink," Riley said. "I'll leave the official naming to the people who adopt them."

"You're going to let them go?" Hallie turned to Riley, her whisper brimming with wonder and hope.

Riley smiled and nodded. "Yes, at nine weeks. As much as I'd love to, I can't keep them. Can you imagine maintaining these gorgeous old hardwood floors with a house full of dogs? They'd be destroyed. I'm renting the place from the Coopers, and while they've been incredibly understanding, I imagine five pets would be pushing their good natures too far."

Hallie cradled the female in the pink collar to her heart. "Are they already spoken for?"

"Uh-oh, Trey." Joe snickered as he cocked his head toward the obviously smitten woman. "Looks like somebody's got fur-baby fever."

"Not yet," Riley assured her. "If you're interested, let me know, and I'll reserve one for you."

"Jake would love a dog," Eden said to her husband.

Joe shot Riley a look. "Oh man, look what you've done."

Riley chuckled at his look of dismay. "Go home and talk about it. There's no need to decide right away."

Sam cleared his throat. "You don't want to wait *too* long." The look on his face said he was clearly enjoying adding to his friend's discomfort. "With only four to choose from, I think they'll go pretty fast."

"What are you doing?" Joe cuffed him. "Trying to start a riot?"

Riley laughed. "I promise I didn't invite you over to ambush you. I just wanted some playmates for the dogs. Once we've exhausted them, we can head into the kitchen for coffee. I made a batch of snickerdoodles this afternoon, although I confess I'm nervous about bringing them out with a professional in our midst."

Eden gave her a warm smile. "I love snickerdoodles. And food always tastes better when someone else makes it."

It didn't take long to wear out the puppies. When the last one collapsed into a sleepy heap, they returned them to the pool and reconvened in the kitchen for refreshments. The women clustered in one group around the table while the men congregated in the opposite corner.

Talk in the ladies' circle centered on jobs and clothes and men. Both Eden and Hallie were kind and funny—the type of people she'd be proud to call friends.

"I've got to stop before I explode." Eden popped the last bit of cookie into her mouth and pushed away from the table. "Riley, your snickerdoodles are amazing. If you ever get tired of teaching and crime fighting, I'm always looking for a talented baker."

Hallie laughed. "Weren't you listening at the meeting tonight? She can't leave the school. Who'd protect the kids?"

Riley shook her head. "I think Sam's got things pretty well under control."

By then the men had wandered over in their direction. Sam scooped the last cookie off the plate in the center of the table and took an enormous bite before tilting his head to give her an assessing look. "I might be willing to take you on as backup. We make a pretty good team."

Trey yawned and wrapped an arm around Hallie's shoulders. "I hate to be a party pooper, but my day started early, and I'm beat. I think it's time to say goodnight."

Joe nodded. "We need to pick up Jake at Mary Jo's before it gets too late."

Riley's smile encompassed the group. "Thank you for coming."

"This was fun," Joe said. "We should get together again."

"You're always welcome here." Riley leaned down to scratch Shadow's neck. "Shadow and I appreciate your help with the puppies."

Eden had gathered their coffee cups and carried them to the sink. "Next time we'll bring Jake, if it's okay."

Riley nodded. "I'd love to have him."

She and Sam escorted the others to the front door. After they'd said their goodbyes, a surprisingly lengthy process for people who would likely see each other in a day or two, they stood side by side on the front porch and waved the couples out to their cars.

"That went well." He turned to her and smiled. "Thanks again for inviting everyone over."

"I enjoyed it. Your friends are really nice people." She lowered her hand as their taillights disappeared. "Do you think they got the message about us?"

"I'm cautiously optimistic." He glanced at his watch. "It's late. I guess I need to be going too."

As tired as she was, she hated to see him leave. She probably wouldn't see him again until the night of the festival. "Thank you for taking me to the meeting tonight."

"It was my pleasure." He trotted down the stairs, then paused to wave. "Good night."

Her heart did a sad little dive. He hadn't made it to the end of the property, and she already missed him. "Wait!"

He stopped and turned back, a puzzled look on his face.

"I know you're busy, but if you have any free time, Shadow and I would love it if you came by, you know, to help with the puppies."

A wide grin spread across his face. "I'm always happy to serve and protect. Good night, Riley. See you soon."

# CHAPTER TEN

Maybe letting the puppies out of the crate wasn't the best idea. The first graders were already hyped up on sugar from their class party earlier in the day. Adding canines to the candy rush boosted the noise and energy to an unprecedented level. Though she'd closed the classroom door, Riley feared everyone in the building could hear the pulsing excitement.

"Noah, come back to the circle, please."

He turned to her, his expression angelic. "Blue was trying to get away, Miss Vreeland. I had to catch him."

From his position on the other side of the group, Sam pushed to his feet. "I'll get Blue. Noah, you have a seat."

She shot Sam a smile of gratitude. Once again, she was in his debt. No way she could have pulled off today's surprise without his help. When she'd told him her plan to bring in the puppies for their much-anticipated visit, he offered to go by her house, round the dogs up into their travel crate, and deliver them to her classroom after lunch.

Having their beloved Officer Sam and four wiggling puppies stop by for the afternoon filled their already-full first-grade cups of joy to overflowing.

Noah rejoined the group. "Can they stay here until it's time to go home?"

Riley nodded. "Yes, but they'll have to go back in the crate so they won't have an accident."

She ignored the ensuing potty humor, knowing no self-respecting seven-year-old could resist.

"Are you going to keep the puppies when they're grown-up?" Chris asked.

Riley shook her head. "No. When they're a little older, I'll find families for them."

His narrow shoulders drooped with his heavy sigh. "I wish I could have one."

She bit back her own sigh. She wished he could too. She knew he'd been seeing the school counselor since the incident and he seemed good, but who knew what scars the little boy bore? Dogs seemed to have a way of healing deep emotional hurts.

She breathed a prayer that God would make a way.

"Let's take some pictures before I put them in their crate." She pulled out her cell phone and snapped some shots of the group. "Okay, everybody, back to your seats. We've got less than an hour before dismissal, and I want each of you to draw a picture of yourself in your costume so I can send them with the photos to Mrs. Cooper."

While the students returned to their desks, she and Sam rounded up the dogs and stuffed their protesting bodies into the carrier.

Their gazes locked over the container, and she smiled. "Thank you again. You saved the day. There's no way I could have accomplished this without you."

He met her smile with an answering dimple. "I wouldn't have missed it. There's nothing greater than a mess of kids and dogs mixing it up." He glanced at the crate. "How are you planning to get them home?"

"Honestly, I haven't thought that far ahead." She considered the enormous beige plastic carrier for a moment then shrugged. "I suppose I'll drag the crate out to the car and away we'll go."

He frowned. "I want you to know I'm not taking anything away from your superpowers when I say you'll never be able to lift them." He ran a hand across his jaw. "I'm leaving now. Why don't you let me take them with me? I'll put them in the pen in your backyard. It's cool enough this afternoon. They'll be fine out there."

"But I told the kids—"

"I'll handle it." Officer Bossy turned to the class. "Okay, everyone, listen up. The puppies just told me they wanted one more ride in my squad car, so I'm going to take them with me now."

Chris's eyes went wide. "Do you speak dog language?"

Sam kept a straight face as he nodded modestly. "Just the basics."

Such was the power of Officer Sam that instead of being disappointed their four-legged guests were making a premature departure, the children were delighted the puppies would be riding in style.

"Can you turn on your siren for them?" Adria asked.

"That would scare them," Olivia said. "Maybe you could just turn on your lights."

Justin shook his head. "That'd be worse. My dad says when the police turn on their lights, it scares him to death."

Olivia pushed her glasses up on her nose. "That's because your dad is a crazy driver."

Sam's eyes danced as he shared a look with Riley and laughed. "Maybe I'll leave the lights and siren off, just in case."

After he'd hefted the carrier to his chest and started toward the door, Riley waved. "Thank you for coming, Officer Sam."

He turned to smile at them. "It's my pleasure. I hope I'll see all of you tonight at the Fall Festival. And I'll be back in a couple of weeks with a new book to read to you."

Once he'd made it to the hall, outside the range of the kids, he sent Riley a wink. "I'll see you later."

That evening, Riley frowned as she studied her reflection in the bathroom mirror. What had seemed like a good idea a week ago now seemed . . . tacky. Nearly everyone she'd spoken to said they were dressing up tonight. Young and old seemed genuinely delighted with the idea of donning a costume. Her—not so much. She wasn't the masquerade type.

In an attempt to be a good sport and enter into the spirit of the event, she'd ordered the basic components for a modified Wonder Woman costume off the internet and had them delivered to the house. Wearing jeans and a T-shirt emblazoned with the Wonder Woman logo, a shiny red cape, and gold tiara resting against her forehead below her teased hair, she figured she would be recognizable as the iconic action hero without stepping into the ridiculous.

The golden vinyl gauntlets she'd snapped onto her wrists gleamed as she gave her reflection a bracing two thumbs up. She gritted her teeth. Now all she had to do was work up the courage to leave the house dressed like this.

No way around it. She was meeting Sam at their booth at five o'clock, and he'd be expecting the costume.

The Wonder Woman theme had been partially Sam's idea. They'd been laughing over her celebrity status with the townspeople since her scuffle with Hector, and when it came time to choose a costume for tonight, he'd suggested a superhero. Through the process of elimination—Riley preferred to be a female crime fighter and refused to wear a slinky bodysuit—she decided on Wonder Woman.

She sat on the edge of the tub to put on her sneakers. Because Sam would be working the event in an official capacity, he'd be wearing his uniform. Funny, the thought didn't bother her like it used to. The sight of a badge and a gun no longer sent her into a panic as it had only a few weeks ago, probably because the more time she spent time with Sam, the more her memories of Ron faded.

She hoped, one day, to forget him completely. She looked forward to taking back the life he'd stolen from her.

The thought of regaining her old life brought an odd little hitch to her heart. Sadness? Where did that come from? Since her arrival in August, she'd been eagerly anticipating her return to Oklahoma City. She had a home, friends, and a life there. Her history was there. Village Green was only a stopping place, a shelter in the storm until she could get rid of Ron.

It never occurred to her she'd miss the things she found here. But then, she hadn't expected to love her school, her rental house, or the town. She hadn't planned to make such deep connections in her temporary arrangement. She hadn't hoped to make such good friends. Mary Jo, Mrs. Peeper, and Sam, especially Sam—they'd all made a huge impact in her life in a very short time. How would she say goodbye?

She rolled her eyes at her reflection and switched off the light. No point in mourning a loss that hadn't happened. Mrs. Cooper remained ill, and Riley had a job to do. Until she knew she was safe, she wouldn't be returning to Oklahoma.

"Shadow, I'm leaving." The corner of her cape brushed along the dog's back as Riley bent to pet her. "Do you want to stay inside while I'm gone or hang out with the kids?"

The dog followed her to the kitchen door in what Riley assumed was an indication of her desire to join the puppies in the backyard. Riley grabbed her purse from the counter and locked the back door before opening the gate to the temporary pen Sam had constructed and scooting Shadow in. She relatched the gate before the excited puppies could escape. "Behave yourselves. Mind your mother. I'll be home by ten."

As per Sam's instructions, Riley parked in the small, paved lot at the police station and walked to the Green. A slight breeze rich with the scent of autumn leaves stirred the hem of her cape. The weatherman predicted a clear night with a low of sixty-five degrees, perfect weather for a fall festival.

She crossed the street and stepped onto the sidewalk. The town had been named for the grassy two-block-long park situated in the middle of the downtown area. Enclosed by an ancient wrought iron fence and dotted with clusters of enormous trees and lush flower beds, the Green was a great place to gather and enjoy the outdoors.

She entered at the first gate and crunched along the gravel path toward the north end of the Green where booths were placed in a semicircle that followed the contours of the fence. A huge white canopy stood opposite the booths, set up with tables and chairs.

Here the smell of leaves was overlaid with the tantalizing aroma of fair food—popcorn and cotton candy and hot grease. Pastor Dale had announced on Sunday that the church ladies' booth would be offering their usual assortment of drinks and snacks, and one of the Sunday school classes would be serving hot dogs and hamburgers. She could hear the low chatter of men at the grills and caught a whiff of the smoky charcoal fires.

Slowing, she scanned the people in and around the booths, looking for Sam. There. Her heart did a fluttery little stutter of recognition as she spotted him. He must have been watching for her because he waved and headed in her direction.

"You made it." He met her a few yards from the booths, his grin wide enough to produce bracketing dimples. "You look Wonder-ful."

Arms extended, she turned a slow full circle before stopping with her legs braced and fists raised in a classic pose.

"Criminals everywhere are shaking in their boots. Speaking of which, where are yours?" He lowered his focus to her legs. "Doesn't Wonder Woman sport a pair of knee-high boots?"

Riley sent him a dampening frown. "She also wears some sort of bathing suit thingy. Not exactly the style for a first-grade teacher trying to set a good example."

"Good point. And while I admire your modesty, I believe you would really rock the boots."

His long look of frank admiration caused her face to heat. Resisting the sudden urge to fan herself, she cleared her throat. "Thank you, I think."

"Is that business casual for cops?" Instead of his crisp navy uniform shirt and slacks, he wore a snug navy T-shirt printed with a city logo on the front and POLICE on the back, a matching POLICE ball cap, faded jeans, and black sneakers. Something about his posture and bearing, even in faded jeans and a T-shirt, projected competency and command.

He flicked a downward glance. "Since they wouldn't let me wear a costume, I opted for comfortable." He must have caught the grin she tried to hide. "What?"

"You reminded me of a superhero when I first met you."

"No way. Let me guess." He made a clowning show of flexing his muscles while flicking back an imaginary lock of long hair. "Thor, right?"

She looked at his short, dark hair and snorted a laugh. "Yeah. That was my second thought. Actually, you reminded me of Captain America."

His comically crestfallen expression telegraphed his disappointment. "I was hoping you'd say someone cool—like Spiderman."

"I wasn't aware you had web-spinning abilities."

"I don't have a shield to throw either."

"True, but you do have those boyish good looks and all-American vibe about you."

He wrinkled his nose, making it clear those weren't the manly qualities he wanted to hear. "Thank you, I think. Hey, come see our spot." He grabbed her hand and led her to the very last booth, at the far end of the semicircle.

He'd taken her hand for expediency, nothing romantic about being towed across the field, and yet, somehow, his touch made her feel tingly. Flutters and tingles and breathlessness for her friend? She must have her tiara on too tight. Whatever, his hand was warm and strong, and she felt the loss when he released her.

She glanced around. "How come we're out here in no-man's-land?"

"Insurance against misfired darts. By sticking us on the end—no pun intended—an overzealous thrower is less likely to puncture someone."

"Makes sense." She glanced up at the sturdy wooden structure, fitted with two sides and a back and draped with heavy canvas. Tucked inside were several panels of drywall with rows of balloons tacked to them. "This is very impressive."

She stepped back a couple of feet to study the rest of the booths, nearly a dozen, all similarly constructed with two-by-four frames and finished out with an overhanging roof and walls made of canvas. "Somebody went to a lot of work to set this up. It must have taken hours."

He moved to her side and sank his hands in his pockets. "Nine hours, counting the tent over the dining area."

"I take it you helped. Although I have no idea when you found the time."

"Me and about twenty-five other dedicated citizens. We started it yesterday morning and finished it this afternoon."

"Wow. That's a lot of manpower. You people take your festival seriously."

He nodded. "Village Green was in trouble after the interstate passed us by. Showy events to put us on the map are part of the effort to keep us from disappearing."

"Is it working?" She hated to think of the quirky little town fading into oblivion.

"I'm going to say yes since we lured you here with an article about Village Green's charms." His eyes searched hers. "That's why you're here, right?"

*She should tell him about Ron.* By now she knew him well enough to know he'd help her. Cop or not, his loyalty would be with her. But the timing wasn't right. She dropped her gaze to break the connection. "It was a combination of things. I needed to get away. I saw the article, and there was a job opening at the school." She shrugged. "Everything just fell into place."

To his credit, he didn't push for answers. "Are you glad you made the move?"

"Absolutely. I would never have met Shadow otherwise." She laughed when the smile slid from his mouth. "And the people I've met here are okay too."

"Gee, thanks."

She took an unhurried moment to study his face, cataloging the dark eyes that tended to sparkle with humor, the strong nose and jaw which spoke of power and gentleness. When had he become so important to her? "Earlier today I was thinking of the friends I've made here and how I'll miss them when I'm gone."

His brows shot up. "What gone?"

"I'm only a temporary resident of Village Green, remember? I've got the job and house for a year, then I'll head back to Oklahoma."

"You miss it." His words carried both understanding and resignation.

She nodded slowly. "Less and less. But I have friends there, and I need to decide what to do with my parent's house . . ."

The dimples were back. "We'll just have to find a reason for you to stay."

"We've got the first and last shift." Sam pointed to the sign-up sheet he'd tacked on the side of the booth. "I figure in between them we can check out the rest of the festival and grab something to eat. I don't know about you, but I'm starved."

"Sounds good." She bent to place her handbag on the ground between the dartboard and canvas wall.

Superhero was a good look for her. Of course, she looked great in everything. School-teacher neat, going-to-church polished, even dog-delivery tousled, she'd managed to look like a million bucks.

She'd rattled him with her talk about leaving. He knew her job and rental house were just a one-year commitment, but he'd never thought it through to its logical conclusion—that she'd actually *leave* at the end of the year.

Up until now, he'd been doing a great job of keeping things in perspective. They were just friends, after all. But that didn't mean he was willing to let her go. She'd come to mean the world to him—as a friend. As she'd let her guard down enough to spend time with him, their relationship had deepened. They had so much in common. Both believers, they loved Jesus and kids and dogs and shared a bone-deep commitment to serving the people in their spheres.

He couldn't pinpoint the exact moment she'd become the best part of his days.

Darn good thing he was a man of his word, because he was just that close to falling in love with her.

Which would be stupid. Criminally stupid.

"Did you blow up all these balloons?" she asked.

He shook his head. "I brought a couple of pumps to the police station. Anytime anyone had a free moment, they inflated a couple and stuck them in a trash bag." He pointed to the four huge bags behind the drywall. "We should have enough to last us all night, but I brought the pumps and extra balloons, just in case."

Activity on the Green increased as costumed children and adults arrived in a steady stream. Inside the booths, workers finished setting up. The chatter on Sam's radio indicated the on-street parking was already full, and they were directing people to leave their cars at the church.

Hallie walked up, dressed as a princess, the ever-present camera in her hands. "Hi, y'all. Can I get a picture of the two of you in front of the dartboard for the website?"

Riley shook her head and took a step back. "I think I'll sit this one out."

Hallie frowned. "You've got to be in it. It's your booth."

"But I . . ." Riley's expression took on the troubled look Sam had seen in the past.

"Don't worry. Your costume's great." Focused on her job, Hallie seemed to miss the genuine distress in Riley's voice. She motioned for the two of them to stand side by side in front of the booth and snapped a shot before Riley could protest further. "Perfect. Thanks."

"Camera shy?" Sam asked after Hallie trotted off toward the gazebo where they'd be kicking off the festivities at any moment.

Riley dropped her gaze. "Not exactly. I, uh, I just don't want to be immortalized with bouffant hair and a tiara." She chewed her lip as she looked toward Hallie's retreating form. "Maybe I can talk her out of posting it."

He set his hands on her shoulders and waited until she lifted her eyes to meet his. "You look great. Beautiful, actually. But if you're worried about the picture going viral, don't." He added wattage to his smile to ease her concerns. "Anything posted on our city website will not lead to fame and international renown. With our miniscule population, very few people will ever see it."

Some of the anxiety in her eyes seemed to fade, and she nodded. "A person would have to be intentionally looking at the website to see them."

"Exactly." He gave her shoulders a quick squeeze before releasing her. "Your alter ego will remain our secret. You're safe."

The sound system squawked. From their vantage point, they could see the mayor fiddling with the microphone inside the gazebo.

"Welcome to our second annual Fall Festival," he said.

The crowd clustered at the base of the platform applauded.

The mayor raised his hands for silence. "Let me mention a few important details about tonight's event, then I'll turn the microphone over to Pastor Dale for a quick prayer. Once he's finished, you all get out there and enjoy the party."

Five minutes later, a line of kids with their parents formed in front of the dart booth.

Chris, dressed as a pint-sized policeman, and Darcie, wearing a cat-eared headband, fronted the line. "Hey, Officer Sam. Miss Vreeland."

Sam tapped the plastic badge over Chris's heart. "Nice costume, dude."

While Riley kept the others at a safe distance, Sam handed Chris three darts and showed him where to stand. "For every balloon you pop, you collect a prize."

Chris took several practice swings with the dart before he released it. *Pop.*

"Well done, my man." He clapped the beaming child on the shoulder. "Let's see if you can do it again."

Darcie moved to Sam's side while Chris warmed up for his next shot. "I wanted to thank you for connecting me with Pastor Dale."

Sam nodded. "You're welcome. How's it going?"

"Really well. He's a great teacher." She lowered her voice. "Who knew a guy that old would be so good with computers."

Sam chuckled. "He loves to quote a scripture about being a tree planted by a river that bears fruit in all seasons."

"I don't know about trees, but he's amazing. And he gave me his old laptop. To keep." Darcie was wide-eyed over the unexpected largesse. "Said he didn't need it anymore. He agrees with you that an office job with benefits might be better for me and Chris. He helped me fill out several online applications and send them off. We'll see if anything comes of them."

Sam angled away from the dartboard to face her. "I'm really proud of you, Darcie."

She dipped her chin and hiked up her shoulders, clearly uncomfortable with the praise. "I haven't done anything yet."

"I disagree. Anytime you put yourself out there to learn something new, you're doing something."

Chris popped a balloon with each dart. Sam pointed to the basket of prizes placed at a safe distance from the target. "Help yourself to three. And great job."

Sam got the next kid queued up and handed her the darts while Chris selected his items, all chocolate, and dropped them in his bag.

"Hey, Miss Vreeland. My mom says we can think about getting one of the puppies."

Riley looked to Darcie who nodded her affirmation. "Do you have a favorite?"

"Yes, ma'am. I especially like the one with the green collar."

"Then I'll put your name on her." She smiled at his mother. "No obligation. You two talk about it and get back to me. They still have a few more weeks before they can be adopted."

"Thank you." They walked away with a wave.

The thirty-minute shift passed in a blur. Darts were so popular that it wasn't uncommon for a kid to take a turn and immediately head to the back of the line to do it again. When their replacements, Mrs. Peeper and Sarah, arrived in matching overalls and County Elementary T-shirts, Sam took a minute to change out the popped balloons on the board. Riley held the darts—insurance against him being skewered—explained the rules and showed them where the extras were stored.

He took a last quick look around to be sure everything was in order. "You two good? Can we go?"

"Sure. Have fun." Mrs. Peeper motioned them off with a sly smile and a sweep of her hand. "We've got this."

By now the sun had set, blanketing the surrounding downtown area in evening shadows. The part of the Green used for the festival was illuminated to near daylight by tall stands of lights powered by humming generators.

"What do you want to do first?" Sam placed his hand at Riley's back and directed her through the line of waiting kids.

She glanced around. "Let's eat."

"Good choice. This way." He took the lead, calling out greetings to friends and neighbors as they wove a path through the milling crowd to the church ladies' booth.

"Hi, Sam. Riley." The choir director waved them over to where she stood behind a table. "What can I get you?"

He took a moment to scan the menu written on a whiteboard. "What are you recommending?"

"Everything's good." She glanced over her shoulder toward a huge cast-iron grill chuffing billows of smoke. "Mason Ryder is cooking his famous hamburgers. Those are always a favorite."

He turned to Riley. "Are you up for a burger?"

She nodded. "Sounds great. And sweet tea to drink, please."

"Same for me, Mrs. Beasley." He pulled out his wallet and handed her a couple of bills.

She made his change out of a plastic cash drawer. "Let me get your drinks, then you go find a seat under the canopy. We'll bring your food out to you as soon as it's ready."

She handed Styrofoam cups to them. "It was so nice to see you in church, Riley."

Riley smiled. "Thank you. I enjoyed it."

"We've got a place for you in the choir if you're interested." Mrs. Beasley waved them off. "Enjoy your dinner."

They exchanged more greetings as they headed to the dining area and sat at an empty table covered with a clean orange plastic cloth.

"I don't think we passed a single person who you didn't call by name." Riley took the chair across from his and eyed him with a look of wonder. "Do you know *everyone*?"

He chuckled. "It'd be more impressive if Village Green wasn't so small."

Leaning back against the folding chair, her gaze swept the area. "Tonight reminds me of a Hallmark movie—you know, lots of families hanging out for some wholesome small-town entertainment. It's nice."

He didn't know Hallmark movies, but he liked that she could see his town, warts and all, in a positive light. One more tally on the ever-growing list of great things about Riley.

*Oh no.* Out of the corner of his eye he saw Jane Ryder, premier small-town matchmaking busybody, bearing down on them, a plastic plate with a burger in each hand. *Tough to put a positive spin on Jane.*

Mrs. Ryder stopped alongside their table and smiled. "Together again, I see." Her brows rose as her expression turned coy. "Another work assignment, no doubt."

He stood. "Yes, ma'am. Ms. Vreeland and I were tasked with managing the joint police/elementary school booth. We're taking a short break before our next shift."

She slid a plate in front of each of them. "You know, it's not unheard of for a single man and a single woman who spend a lot of time together to develop feelings for each other." She waggled her eyebrows suggestively. "Romantic feelings."

Polite smile in place, he waited until Jane headed back to the food tent before returning to his seat. He leaned toward Riley to whisper, "Do they have busybodies in Hallmark movies?"

Riley laughed. "She's relentless."

"She's not subtle, that's for sure." He sighed. "She means well—"

"She means well," Riley said at the very same time.

Their eyes met in the shared joke, and they laughed.

The burger was delicious, the best he'd ever eaten. Partially because Mason was a genius at the grill, and mostly because being with Riley made everything better. He didn't know why he continued to deny the truth staring him in the face. He had it bad for Riley. Real bad.

They ate in relative peace. Relative in that while everybody in town seemed to feel the need to stop by their table to greet them, no one besides Jane resorted to eyebrow waggling and overt match-making. There were plenty of covert looks and smiles—he hoped Riley missed them.

He wiped his mouth and set his napkin on the table. "That was amazing. What's next?"

She tilted her head while giving his question some thought. "Something sweet. Let's head over to Eden's booth and win a cup-cake for dessert."

They carried their trash to the can by the exit. This time when they crossed the Green, he kept his hand to himself. He didn't want to give anyone the idea—himself included—that their relationship was anything other than friendship.

"Hey, y'all." Eden waved as they joined the back of the line at her booth.

The cupcake walk was basically a game of musical chairs. Eden placed a cardboard cutout of a cupcake under two of the eight folding chairs set in a row. Eight participants walked around the chairs to circus-themed music. When the music stopped, everyone scrambled to the closest chair. Those with a cupcake beneath them collected their prize, a real cupcake from one of the bakery boxes displayed on the table. Everyone else hurried around to the back of the line to try again. Pretty lame. He'd have been embarrassed to join the child's game if over half the players weren't adults.

The queue shuffled forward along the trampled grass as the next eight people took their places. Jim and Jessica Baker and their daughter Olivia stood in line directly in front of them. Jim turned when he noticed Sam and extended a hand. "Hey, man. How's it going?"

"Great." Sam gave him a firm shake. "Perfect night for a festival."

Jim tapped his daughter on the shoulder. "Look, Olivia. Officer Sam and your teacher are behind us."

Olivia pushed her glasses up on her nose. "Hi, Officer Sam. Wow, Miss Vreeland, you look pretty. Are you a princess too?"

"Thank you. Actually, I'm supposed to be Wonder Woman."

"Probably be easier to tell if she'd worn boots," Sam suggested under his breath.

Riley gave him a discreet elbow to the ribs. "Wonder Woman is a superhero."

"Speaking of heroes, we heard about what happened up at the school." Jim frowned. "We're grateful you were there to stop that guy from messing with Darcie and Chris."

"I just slowed him down." She pointed to Sam. "He did the actual stopping."

"She conked him on the head, Dad, and then Officer Sam cuffed him."

"I heard." He smiled at his daughter before turning back to Riley. "I hope you know that kind of stuff just doesn't happen around here. We've got a nice, safe town thanks to Sam and the rest of the police force."

"I'm a huge fan of Village Green," she assured him.

Jim nudged Sam and smiled. "I'm sure Sam's glad to hear that."

After Jim turned his back, Sam mouthed the words. "They mean well."

Riley snorted a laugh.

Winning a pair of cupcakes wasn't as easy as it appeared. It took three tries to nab the first one, a red velvet cake with a thick swirl of icing. Time ticked away with each tedious pass around the chairs. There was only an hour before their second shift began.

Riley whispered, "I'm done. If I have to listen to that song one more time, I won't be responsible for my actions."

Sam laughed. "If you're willing, we can share this one."

"Deal."

They moved as far as they could from the music, and finding a small patch of unoccupied grass, they stopped and turned their backs to the booths. He pulled the wrapper off their dessert and frowned. "I'm not sure I can break it in half without making a mess."

"No problem." Hand on his, she guided the cupcake to his mouth. "Since you won it, you get the first bite."

He sank his teeth into it. "Oh, man. This is fantastic." Following her example, he held the remainder to her lips. "Try it."

Her lashes lowered as she took a bite. "Mmm. That might be the best thing I've ever eaten."

"I think it's the icing," he lied. It could be the cardboard cutout, and he'd swear it was delicious. Standing mere inches from Riley and eating from her hand was strangely intimate. And exciting. He ate half of the remaining cupcake before feeding her the last bit.

"Oh wait, you've got a little icing..." Riley reached up and swept a gentle fingertip over the corner of his mouth. "Got it."

His stomach tightened. He raised his hand to the suddenly sensitive spot on his lip.

She lifted her eyes to his. "What do you want to do now?"

*I want to kiss you.*

Whoa, buddy. Step away from the lips. Kissing would definitely exceed the posted limits of friendship. Dragging his gaze from her face, he cleared his throat and glanced at his watch. "We've got some time before our next shift. Do you want to look around?"

By eight o'clock, the composition of the crowd had changed. Parents shepherding little princesses and tiny heroes through the activities had taken them home to bed, leaving the last hour of the festival to the older kids. Adults visited with friends under the canopy while their teens wandered in laughing clusters.

He and Riley strolled under the lights, close enough to the booths to see and hear the excitement, far enough away for a sense of privacy. Their shoulders bumped as they walked and talked. He could have moved two inches away and broken the occasional connection, but he didn't. It was foolish, but he liked her touch, even if it was an accident.

Their final shift at the booth went far too quickly for Sam. By ten o'clock, they finished up for the night, and he followed her home. She'd assured him it wasn't necessary, but he'd insisted. It was late. Somebody needed to be certain she got in okay. And he'd never say no to a little extra time with her, even from a distance.

They agreed he'd pull up in front of her house while she parked in the garage and entered through the kitchen. She'd flicker the porch lights, signaling she was in, and he'd leave.

Shortly after the garage door went down, the front door opened, and Riley stepped out. When she descended the stairs and angled across the lawn in his direction, he hopped out of the truck and met her mid-yard. "Everything okay?"

The streetlight glinted off the golden band on her forehead as she nodded. "I just wanted to say thank you again. Tonight was really fun."

His gaze locked with hers. "I thought so too."

He didn't know how long they stood there, in the middle of the yard, smiling at each other, but in those few moments everything in his world was right.

At last, she shrugged. "Well, good night."

"I'm not leaving with you standing out here in the dark." He placed a hand on her cape-covered shoulder. "Come on, I'll walk you to the door."

They climbed the steps together and he opened the screen door for her. "Get on in there."

She entered and turned immediately, tilting her face up to his. "Thank you, again."

He kissed her.

He shouldn't have done it. He should have given her a wave and trotted back to his truck. He hadn't meant to do it. It just happened.

He'd been memorizing the way the shadows played on her skin and the soft look in her eyes when she smiled. Suddenly his attention was one hundred percent on her mouth. He couldn't look away any more than he could stop the slow magnetic pull toward her. He leaned in, and she lifted her face to meet his. Her eyes fluttered shut, and he touched his mouth to hers. He'd meant it to be a quick peck, but when her hand stole up to rest over his heart, he pressed in for more, deepening it to a thorough, earth-moving, heart-pounding kiss.

A nearby dog barked, and the spell was broken.

Sam straightened and blew out a breath. "Wow. Didn't mean to go there."

Hand on the wall for support, Riley blinked. "Wow."

He needed to say something. But what? He couldn't apologize. The unexpected kiss was the truest, most authentic expression of his feelings. "I know you want to be friends. I support that. It's just . . . Don't worry. I promise. This won't change anything."

# CHAPTER ELEVEN

It changed everything.

One night and one incredible kiss turned Riley's world upside down and her intentions to dust. Suddenly just being his friend wasn't enough. She wanted more. And judging by the kiss, Sam did too.

Even the best of friends didn't kiss like that.

Two days later she was still reeling. "It was . . . transcendent." She tried to explain to Shadow what she didn't fully understand herself. The whole night had been magical. Spending time with Sam was always wonderful, but Friday night with him had been extra special. The two of them together felt connected. Complete. And when he kissed her . . .

"Don't give me that look. I know what you're thinking, but this is not about hormones, although I admit, there were plenty of them." She lowered her mascara wand to narrow her eyes at the dog sitting patiently at her feet. "Anyone with a litter fathered by who knows who is not in a position to judge."

She turned back to the mirror. "The point is this is more meaningful than simple attraction." She frowned. "At least, *I* think it is."

With each passing moment, doubts nibbled away at the edges of her certainty. Maybe she got carried away by the celebration and the moonlight and the community spirit—was there such a thing as the Hallmark effect? Maybe she was reading too much into what was intended as a simple, goodnight kiss.

Maybe she *had* worn her tiara too tight.

No amount of doubt could make her believe Sam was simply hitting on her. She knew him too well as her friend to believe he was a closet Casanova, waiting to seduce the unwary. Ron had put a real dent in her confidence about her judgment, but even coming from her new perspective, she knew deep down that Sam was a man of integrity. The real deal.

She puckered up and applied a coat of creamy rose lipstick. "I'll feel better once I talk to him."

They hadn't spoken since The Kiss. He'd sent a brief text last evening, checking to see if she'd be in church today, but that had been their only communication. Of course, that was normal. They didn't talk every day. He'd said the kiss wouldn't change anything. Apparently, for him it hadn't.

To be fair, she'd been the one who was adamant they keep things casual between them. The question now was—would he be open to change?

Shadow trailed her into the closet. "I need something special to wear today," Riley said. "A breakthrough outfit." Hanger by hanger she pushed through her options before pulling out a pale blue dress. "What do you think?"

The dog lay down, sinking her chin on her paws.

"Yeah, too plain." Riley returned the dress to the rod and continued her search. She pulled out a second dress, this one a coppery red with a swishy full skirt. "How about this one?"

Shadow's tongue lolled out.

"You're right. Trying too hard." She hung up the dress. "I'm running out of options here."

Toward the end of the rack, she found a dress she'd picked up on sale at the end of the season and hadn't yet had a chance to wear. Whisper-soft jersey in a rich shade of green that brought out the same color in her eyes, it was the perfect let's-take-this-relationship-to-the-next-level dress.

She pulled it over her head, the silky fabric gliding over her curves, the hem falling at her knees. She slipped on a pair of taupe heels and studied her reflection in the full-length mirror on the back of the closet door. "Be honest. What do you think?"

Shadow hopped up, wagging her tail.

"I agree." She gave the dog a good scratch behind the ears. "We've got ourselves a winner."

An hour later, Riley entered the back of the sanctuary and paused, scanning the semi-full pews for a place to sit. Last week, she'd sat with Mary Jo, Eden, and Joe. Now she spotted them about midway up the aisle and started out to join them when she noticed Sam was part of their group this morning.

Just the sight of the back of his head fired up her nerve endings like sparklers on the fourth of July. Schooling her expression to calm, she walked up to the pew and bent slightly to ask, "May I join you?"

Sam sent her a friendly smile, the same one he would give anyone in town, and patted the open space beside him. "Sure. Have a seat."

Mary Jo leaned across the others. "Good morning, dear. I've been hearing all about Friday night. Sounds like it was a huge success."

The five of them spent the time before the service in a hushed discussion of the festival. Riley was proud of her contribution to the conversation, so calm and natural, despite the fact her heart had doubled its pace, and she had to remind herself to breathe.

Though she tried not to look at Sam, she couldn't help peeking at his hand resting on his thigh. She was inordinately aware of every detail of his long, strong fingers and the dusting of dark hair on his forearm. His fragrance, the simple, clean smell she'd always associated with him, scattered her thoughts in a hundred directions.

Sam seemed untouched by this dizzying new awareness. He'd slid over to make room for her on the pew and turned toward her when she spoke, but his behavior was as it had always been. Friendly. Casual. Unchanged.

The organist began the first hymn, and the congregation stood. Sam pulled the hymnal from the pew back and flipped to the correct page. He angled toward her, holding the book so they could share it.

"How am I going to concentrate with you beside me?" His light-as-air whisper ruffled the hair by her ear and every cell in her body.

Her breath caught. Had she heard him correctly? Careful not to attract attention, she turned her head a fraction to study his face. The warm light in his eyes said he felt it too. Joy flooded her.

Face forward, she whispered, "Right back at you."

Despite the pastor's skill with Scripture, Riley didn't hear half of what he said. Her focus was on the man beside her. Separated by only an inch, she was tempted to scoot over and close the distance. As nice as it would be to feel the solid connection of his shoulder pressed to hers, it would also feed the relentless small-town rumor mill. So she sat board straight, eyes on the pastor, hands in her lap, and savored Sam's nearness.

After the final hymn and benediction, they filed out of the sanctuary, Eden toward the nursery to pick up Jake, while the rest of them continued to the front lawn. Trey and Hallie joined them on the grass.

"We're going to Corsicana for lunch." Joe looked from Riley to Sam. "Want to come along?"

Riley glanced at Sam, trying to telegraph her feelings without altering her expression.

"Another time." Sam gave the group an easy smile. "I've got the afternoon shift today, so I need to stay close to home. I'm going to try to talk Riley into keeping me company over lunch at Estelle's."

After another glance at the two of them, Joe's expression became self-conscious. "Oh. Oh right." He turned to the others and said in a too-loud voice, "Sam and Riley are going to Estelle's."

"I guess we could all go—" Trey said.

"No!" Joe, Hallie, and Mary Jo responded in adamant unison.

Trey frowned. "Am I missing some—" Hallie silenced him with a yank of his hand.

"Okay, well, you two have fun. We'll see you later." Joe wrapped one arm around Eden when she arrived with Jake and the other around Mary Jo and herded them toward the parking lot. Trey and Hallie followed at a fast trot.

Riley stood at Sam's side, watching their hasty departure. "That was awkward."

"Not as awkward as going to lunch as one big happy group." He gave her a meaningful look. "I was hoping we could be alone so we could talk."

Her heart did a little flip. "Me too."

"Lunch at Estelle's?"

She nodded. "I'd love it."

"Let's take my truck. We can pick up your car after we eat."

Estelle's had a pretty good crowd by the time Riley and Sam arrived. The owner met them at the door and pointed them toward the back of the restaurant. "The last two booths are open. Why don't you sit there, where it's quieter?"

Riley bit back a sigh. Estelle hadn't wiggled her eyebrows, but her intentions were clear. "Is it just me or is the entire town bent on matchmaking?" she whispered as he led the way.

"Whole town," he confirmed under his breath.

On their short trek to the table, they stopped at least a half dozen times to greet friends or neighbors, many of whom they'd just seen at church. Ever the gentleman, Sam stood until she was seated, then slid onto the bench across from her, his back to the wall.

Estelle approached, carrying a full tray of dishes and glasses. "What can I get you to drink?"

Riley smiled. "Sweet tea, please."

"Same here, Estelle."

"Do y'all need a minute to look over the menu?" She indicated the laminated page wedged behind the napkin dispenser with a lift of her chin. "Today's special is turkey and dressing with mashed potatoes and green beans."

Nerves had prevented Riley from eating breakfast. Now that she was here, with him, her appetite came flooding back. "Yum, I'll have the special."

Sam nodded. "Make that two, please."

The older woman smiled. "Two specials, coming up."

She hadn't been gone more than a minute when Sam started to chuckle.

"What's so funny?"

"Look behind you. You won't believe what Estelle did."

Riley turned and scooted up on her knees to see over the tall backrest. The booth behind them, the one between their table and the restaurant, was now stacked with plates and glasses. She faced him with a frown. "Why would she do that?"

"She's running interference for us. By placing the dishes on the table, the booth looks occupied. No one else will sit there."

She slunk down on the bench and covered her face with her hands. "I'm trying to decide if I'm flattered or mortified."

"Repeat after me. They mean well."

They laughed.

The fading laughter left behind an air of expectancy. Riley took a deep breath and plunged in, ready and yet terrified to initiate the conversation. "Actually, I'm grateful for the privacy. I want to talk to you about Friday night. About the kiss."

He dropped his gaze, his hand kneading the back of his neck. "I need to—"

"—I've given it a lot of thought, and, well, I want more."

Sam's head snapped up and a grin spread slowly over his handsome face. His dark eyes lit with mischievous delight as he swung his legs over the side of the bench and stood. "Come on, then. Let's step outside, and I'll give you all you want."

She swatted his hand. "I'm not talking about kisses."

Still smiling, he lowered back to the bench. "Before I get my hopes up again, mind telling me what exactly it is you're talking about?"

"I'm talking about us." She had a hard time meeting his eyes. "When I first met you, and up until very recently, I told you I wasn't interested in a dating relationship. That I want to be friends."

He bobbed his head. "Yeah."

"I realize I want more than that, if you're willing." Sudden doubts about his status assailed her. Maybe he'd agreed to be friends because that was all he wanted. Maybe he was interested in someone else. "And if you're not dating anyone else, of course."

He folded his hands on the table, eyes locked on hers. "I'm a free agent. So, the kiss changed your mind?"

"Not exactly." Honesty had her adding, "Although you are an excellent kisser."

"Thank you." Grinning, he gestured toward the door. "My offer is still open to step outside—"

She slanted him a chiding look. "Officer Sam, I had no idea you were such a flirt. No, the kiss didn't change my mind so much as it opened my eyes."

He shook his head. "They were closed. I remember it distinctly."

Her cheeks flamed. "What I'm trying to say is I've been attracted to you for some time." She lowered her eyes and blew out a breath. "Wow, this is really awkward."

"It's working for me." By now his smile was so wide, his dimples had dimples.

He was enjoying her squirming. "Okay, Mr. Serve-and-Protect, feel free to help me out here."

He nodded. "How about I admit I've been attracted to you for a while too."

Joy expanded in her chest. She was tempted to stop here and bask in their mutual attraction. But she owed him an explanation. "I've insisted on sticking to friendship because I've let some issues stand in the way of a dating relationship. No more. I'm finished putting my life on hold. If you're willing, I'd like to explore the possibility of us . . ."

He didn't look as surprised as she'd expected. "And those issues. Are they resolved?"

She shook her head. "Not yet. But when you kissed me, I realized you and I could handle them together."

Man, he was crazy about this woman.

He liked her boldness in telling him how she felt, and her blushes as she did it. He liked the way her eyes picked up the green in her dress, and basically everything the dress did for her. He liked her mind and her mouth, the way she thought and the way she kissed, and everything about her from the top of her head to the soles of her high-heeled shoes.

He loved *the possibility of us.*

He'd gone home Friday night afraid he'd blown everything. He had no business kissing her. All Saturday he'd struggled with how he should handle damage control. It wasn't until he'd worried himself sick that he finally took the problem to God. As he prayed, he felt impressed to be honest. Instead of trying to justify his actions, he needed to tell her why he'd done it. What he felt.

The concept of putting it all on the table terrified him.

As much as he hated the potential for looking like a fool, he hated more the idea of messing up their relationship. Of losing her. So, he'd marched himself to church today, hoping and praying she'd be willing to hear him out.

The smile on her face combined with the fact she was willing to sit beside him gave him the courage to speak.

Estelle brought out dinner, setting two glasses of iced tea on the table before sliding a full plate in front of each of them.

"Thank you." He nodded toward the empty table behind Riley. "And not just for the food."

"You aren't the only one who can set up a roadblock." She winked over the top of her reading glasses. "It just seems to me that folks ought to be able to step out occasionally without everyone being up in their business."

"They mean well," he and Riley said as one.

Though she clearly had no idea what the two of them found so funny, she smiled fondly. "Y'all enjoy your lunch. I'll check back in a bit to see if you need refills on your tea."

After Estelle left, he and Riley bowed their heads as he led them in a quick prayer, then devoted a minute or two to concentrated eating.

Riley pointed to her plate with her fork. "This is delicious."

"Estelle does most of the cooking herself."

"I wonder if she gives out recipes. The corn bread dressing is to die for."

By some unspoken, mutual consent, they kept conversation light as they ate. On Sundays, Estelle switched out the music in the restaurant from country to gospel country. Overhead, Alan Jackson sang "How Great Thou Art."

When their plates were nearly clean, Sam put down his fork to give her his undivided attention. "About those issues you mentioned. I'd like to help."

Frowning, she set her fork on her plate and pushed it away, as if the topic spoiled her appetite. "It's actually *an* issue. Singular. A man."

"Old boyfriend?" He tried for neutral, though every muscle clenched.

"Not really. He wanted to be, but I wasn't interested."

Riley focused on some point past his shoulder, arms folded protectively across her middle, as she described meeting this guy, Ron, at her father's funeral and how he'd quickly insinuated himself into her life. "I was in such a fog after my dad died. He was all I had . . ." Her voice broke.

After a beat of silence, she cleared the emotion from her throat. "Ron's attentions seemed kind at first. He was thoughtful and considerate. I even believed he was protecting me when he told my friends I needed time off from them for privacy to grieve. They stepped back, but he didn't. He went from a compassionate, occasional companion to stalker overnight. He was everywhere I was. I couldn't get rid of him. If I hadn't been in such a fog, I'd have noticed the signs sooner."

"What signs?"

"The unnaturally accelerated pace of our relationship was the biggie. We'd known each other two weeks, hardly more than acquaintances, when he told me he loved me." She grimaced. "That's when I had the clarity to see something wasn't right."

"Forgive me, this is going to sound incredibly personal, but did he try to get physical?" Sam couldn't make himself say rape. Hands fisted under the table, he steeled himself against the desire to pound something as he waited for her answer.

She screwed up her face in disgust. "He kissed me once, if you can call having someone smash their mouth against yours a kiss." She shuddered. "He tried to pass it off as though he'd been carried away by passion, but it didn't feel that way. The whole thing felt calculated, as though it had been scripted."

"But he didn't try to force himself on you?"

At last she seemed to grasp the question he couldn't bring himself to ask. "Not sexually. The day I told him I didn't want to see him again, he grabbed me and shook me. The strength he used against me terrified me. It occurred to me that if he chose to overpower me, he . . ." She didn't finish the thought.

She lifted her gaze to Sam. "He apologized immediately, but I saw something in his eyes before he could mask it—a look of such hostility that the hair stood up on the back of my neck. I acted like nothing was wrong, but that was when I decided to run."

"Aw, Riley." He settled for reaching over and laying a hand on hers when what he really wanted to do was scoop her into his arms and hold her tight. "You've been very brave."

She shook her head. Tears welled and spilled over her lashes. "I've been so afraid, looking over my shoulder, wondering when he'd find me. I didn't know what to do. I couldn't talk to anyone about it . . ."

That hurt. He'd thought they were better friends than that. "Why couldn't you talk to me?"

She swept away the moisture on her cheeks, her damp green eyes meeting his squarely. "He's a cop . . ."

Sam heard a buzzing in his ears and felt his stomach drop. Hadn't he suspected something like this? All her questions about police and loyalties began to make sense.

" . . . maybe."

The single-word disclaimer gave him hope. He straightened. "What do you mean, 'maybe'?"

She shrugged. "He told me he'd gone through police academy, that he'd done really well, but there were only a few slots available, and those went to people with political connections. He said he was waiting for the next opening, and then he'd be in."

That didn't sound like any program Sam was familiar with. And this guy didn't sound like a cop. He sounded like a sociopath. "Where did he say he went to academy?"

"Oklahoma City."

"And what's his name? Full name?"

"Ron. Ron Pearson."

Hmm. What were the odds that was his real name? Sam pulled a piece of paper and pen from his shirt pocket. "I hate to ask you to talk about him, but if you'll answer a few questions, I'll check him out. If he was in a police academy anywhere, I'll find him."

She watched him write out the name. "If? You think he was lying?"

"I do. Partially because I don't like to think one of my own would prey on women, but mostly because it sounds like this guy specifically targeted you."

She lifted her gaze to his. "Why?"

Unable to articulate his hunches, he settled for a shrug. "I don't know. It feels wrong. You met this guy, a complete stranger, at your father's funeral, and he immediately assumes the role of close family friend." He stroked his jaw as he pondered the information. "It's not unheard of for predators to troll obituaries looking for someone to scam. You're the last of your family, right?"

She nodded. He was relieved to see her tears had stopped.

Sam continued to work through the problem out loud. "Typically, obituaries list surviving relatives. Your father's column would have mentioned only you. A person looking for a victim prefers someone without friends or family to protect them. Which would explain why he tried to separate you from your friends. Did he ever ask you for money?"

She shook her head. "Never. He seemed to have plenty. He said he did financial planning."

That fit the profile. "Did he offer to handle yours?"

"Yes. Right after the funeral he volunteered to take on any paperwork resulting from my father's death. He said he knew how difficult it was to deal with the details while grieving, and that he'd be happy to handle them for me."

"You didn't let him—"

She gave a derisive snort. "No way. No matter how ingratiating he tried to be, he was still a stranger. I sent everything to the man who's always handled my parents' investments."

"They had investments?"

"A lot, actually. My dad was very interested in finance and the stock market. He said teachers who wanted to retire comfortably had to learn to invest. He taught a class on it at the community college—" She clapped her hand to her forehead. "Oh my gosh!

When Ron introduced himself to me, he mentioned he'd taken my father's class. That's how he knew my dad."

Sam felt a piece fall into place. "So, he sees your dad's obituary and decides to take a gamble that the surviving daughter of a successful investor would pick up a hefty inheritance."

Riley had been nodding along as if his conclusions made sense, when suddenly she stilled, and her face fell. "It sounds reasonable, except when I told him I wasn't interested in his help, he let it drop without argument. Seems like if he was trying to rob me, he'd have persisted."

He wasn't ready to give up on his theory. "Maybe. Or maybe he was biding his time. Waiting you out while he gained your trust. That would explain the accelerated courtship. And why he turned nasty when you tried to give him the boot. He wasn't about to lose you until he got what he came for."

Estelle approached their table. "Y'all want some chocolate pie?"

Riley shook her head. "Not today, thank you. I couldn't eat another bite."

Sam's appetite disappeared with the conversation about Ron. Now that he had somewhere to start, he was eager to begin an investigation. "Just a check, please."

Fifteen minutes later Sam pulled up behind her SUV in the empty church parking lot.

She held out a hand to stop him from shutting down the engine. "You don't need to walk me to my car. You've got to get ready for work."

As if he would let her get into a vehicle he hadn't searched. "Sure I do." He switched off the truck and swung open his door. "How else would I collect a kiss?"

She smiled as he hoped she would. Fact was, she seemed pretty carefree after unburdening her story. He, on the other hand, wouldn't know a moment's peace until he found this guy and got some answers.

Without making a big deal, he scanned the interior of her SUV as they walked to the driver's side. When she unlocked and opened the door, he ducked his head inside for another quick check.

After she slid onto the seat, she turned her eyes to his and rested her palm on his forearm. "I'm sorry I didn't tell you earlier about Ron. It wasn't so much not trusting you as it was not trusting myself."

"Don't apologize." She hadn't trusted him until she was certain she knew where his loyalties lay. Excellent strategy for a woman on the run. "I need to say this again. You are an enormously brave woman, and I am so proud of you."

He waved off the argument he saw brewing on her face. "It took real courage and ingenuity to disappear." He wouldn't say the next words that came to mind, that her quick thinking might have saved her life. "Until I find him, I want you to keep vigilant." Fierce protectiveness sharpened his tone. He took a deep breath and released it, then worked to infuse easiness into his voice. "We're going to work on some defensive skills. I'll do everything in my power to protect you, but since it would cause talk if I camped out in your front yard, I'm depending on you to keep yourself safe when I can't be with you."

Smiling, she bobbed her head. "I can do that, Officer Sam."

"I believe you can, Wonder Woman." He started to close her door. "Text me when you get in."

She stopped it with sole of her sexy shoe. "What about my kiss?"

He'd promised her one as an excuse to walk her to the car but hadn't planned to follow through. In light of their discussion about Ron and his manipulative attempt to woo her, Sam decided to wait until the issue was resolved before kissing her again. He didn't want their relationship to be tangled up with painful memories. Riley was worth the wait.

She must have read his thoughts. "Don't worry. I'd never confuse you with him."

She turned in her seat and lifted her face expectantly.

Tenderness rushed over him, and he cradled her smooth cheek in his palm. He bent and touched his lips to hers with gentle pressure. "I'm not going to linger, but only because it's broad daylight and who knows who's watching."

"Thank you for lunch and listening to me."

"It was my pleasure." He swung her door shut and tapped on her window. When she lowered it, he couldn't resist leaning in for one more kiss. "Don't forget to text me."

He hurried home to change and arrived at the station twenty-five minutes before his shift began.

The clerk at the front desk looked up from her computer. "Hey, Sam. What are you doing here so early?"

He shrugged as he passed. "Just wanted to catch up on a little reading."

Grabbing a soda from the refrigerator, he sat and booted up his computer. First stop, find contact numbers for any police academies in Oklahoma City. He found two. He made a note to call them in the morning and ask them to check their records for Ron Pearson.

The guy was either a wannabe cop or simply smart enough to know that by aligning himself with law enforcement, his mark would be less likely to question his motives.

In the short time he had left before he went on duty, Sam searched the Wanted Persons file and Supervised Release file of the NCIC for any Ron Pearsons fitting Riley's description and living in Oklahoma City. Nothing promising.

Releasing a discouraged breath, he signed off and shut down the computer. Locating this guy would be next to impossible with the little he had to go on.

He leaned back in his chair and scrubbed his hands over his face. Right before they left Estelle's, Riley had suggested that maybe Pearson had given up, moved on. The scenario was possible. Pearson sees she's slipped his hold and decides to find a new mark. A savvy con would take his game to a new locale and start over.

Unless being outsmarted by a 120-pound girl was too much for his ego. Sociopaths generally believed their intellect superior to others. To be beaten by Riley might be just the provocation to put him on the hunt. Especially if he thought the financial prize waiting at the end was worth the effort.

# CHAPTER TWELVE

R iley herded her students down the hall and into the classroom. "Everyone hang up your jackets and get settled in your seats. Officer Sam is coming to read to us this afternoon."

She pulled off her sweater and hung it on the back of her chair before bending to fish a hairbrush from her tote. They'd enjoyed a particularly rowdy game of Red Rover during recess, and even without the benefit of a mirror, she knew she looked as though she'd been dragged backward through the woods.

The sudden swell of voices said it was too late for repairs.

"Look, Miss Vreeland, he's here."

Hand to her hair, she straightened. Tall and handsome, he stood framed in the doorway. Her heart skipped a beat for the man she'd secretly renamed Officer Yummy. "Good afternoon, Officer Sam, you're early today."

"I couldn't wait to see you." Though he extended his arms to include the class, the tone of his voice and look in his eyes said the words were for her alone.

She sent him an answering smile. "We've been looking forward to seeing you too."

Olivia stretched up her hand. "Officer Sam, next week is Thanksgiving, and we have two days off from school."

"That's right. Does anyone have any special plans?"

Riley loved to watch him with the kids. Their interaction was so sweet and natural. He truly listened as they spoke. The man had an enormous capacity for love.

*He'd make a wonderful father.*

That thought and similar ones had been popping into her head since they made the decision to date. With every meal they shared, every long walk they took, even the many hours practicing the self-defense moves he insisted she learn, she fell for him a little more. She'd told him she wanted to go slowly, to take their time getting to know each other, yet she was the one jumping ahead.

Careful not to disturb the lively discussion, she carried a chair to the front center of the room and set it behind him.

"Thank you." He brushed a hand over hers and gave her a secret look, the melting kind that made her legs feel weak. She wobbled to her desk and sat.

Sam took the book from under his arm and displayed it to the class. "If you're ready to listen, I brought a special story to share with you today."

After the room quieted, he continued. "The book was written by Elizabeth Whitney and is titled *I Like Us*." The glance he shot Riley said the story was significant, and she settled in to listen.

As with his previous selections, he'd chosen one in which the characters were cleverly illustrated animals interacting on a human level. Even wiggly kids one week from a holiday were not immune to his soothing baritone. He caught and held their rapt attention from the first page.

"I like going places with you." He held up the book so everyone could see the two monkeys swinging side by side through the trees.

After the class had seen it, he turned to a picture of two elephants sitting next to each other on a sagging couch. "I like staying home with you."

Each page brought the same phrasing with a different pair of animals engaged in a shared activity. The last page read simply "I like us."

He sent her a quick wink over his shoulder before closing the cover and placing the book in his lap.

Message delivered. Her heart puddled like ice cream in August. It took a special man to make story time with a roomful of six- and seven-year-olds romantic.

Sam was the most special man she'd ever known.

She stood and joined the applause of the children. "That was great, Officer Sam. Thank you for coming to read to us." She faced the students. "After we've said our goodbyes, I want each of you to take out a piece of paper and draw a picture of yourself and someone you like doing things with. We'll send them to Mrs. Cooper along with our Thanksgiving card."

They scrambled out of their seats to hug Sam and say goodbye. When everyone had the opportunity to talk with him, she shooed them back to their desks. "Okay, get to work."

She walked Sam just outside the door of the classroom. "Thank you."

"My pleasure." His tone and expression telegraphed that and so much more. "Did you like the book?"

She smiled. "My favorite so far. I especially like us."

"Me too. Dinner still on for tonight?"

"Yes, but don't pick anything up. Let me cook."

He frowned. "Are you sure? After a long day wrangling first graders, you deserve a break."

She lifted a hand to her head, belatedly remembering her recess hair. "My day wasn't nearly as difficult as my hair suggests."

"It's beautiful. So are you." His gaze locked with hers as he took her hand in his for a discreet squeeze. "See you tonight."

That evening Riley hummed as she sautéed the chopped onions, carrots, and celery. In honor of fall, she was trying out her mother's recipe for chicken pot pie. Her dad always said her mom won his heart with the savory dish. She was pretty sure she had Sam's complete devotion, but nothing wrong with solidifying their connection with a dose of comfort food.

She'd teared up when she pulled the lightly stained index card from the old wooden recipe file. With each passing day, she was doing so much better, but occasionally a crashing wave of grief would surprise her. Today was one of those times.

She'd missed the friendship and wisdom of her parents, but the loss seemed more acute as she and Sam grew closer. So many times she regretted he wouldn't have the chance to meet the special people of her past and that they would never know the man who was rapidly becoming her future.

Once the vegetables were soft, she sprinkled flour over them and stirred for a couple minutes until it bubbled. She added the premeasured cream and chicken broth and continued stirring until the mixture resembled rich gravy. Finally, she added the chopped chicken and poured the contents of the skillet into a baking dish. She sent an apology heavenward as she fitted the sheet of pastry over the top, asking her mother to forgive her for using a store-bought pie crust.

After putting the pie in the oven and setting the timer, she hurried to the bathroom to refresh her makeup and hair before Sam arrived. She had just finished buttoning on a clean shirt when she heard his knock.

"Hello." She swung open the door and pushed the storm door aside. "Come in."

He'd changed into a T-shirt and worn jeans. Officer Yummy in civvies was Double Yummy.

He stopped and inhaled deeply. "Umm. Something smells delicious."

"It's chicken pot pie."

"That too." He leaned close and buried his face in her hair. "What I'm smelling is high-dollar shampoo."

She laughed. "That could be me or Shadow."

He gave her a disbelieving look. "You're still using the fancy stuff on the dog?"

"Only on spa days."

He reached down to pet Shadow, who'd followed her to the door. "You certainly landed in high cotton, little lady."

"I'm trying to spoil her a bit before we have to give up her p-u-p-p-i-e-s."

He cocked a brow. "She's spelling now?"

"She's very intelligent." Riley glanced out at the road as she stepped around him to close the door. "I don't see your truck."

"I parked it down at Mary Jo's. She'd asked me to come by this afternoon, and after our visit, I left if there. It's a nice evening for a walk, and since my truck's been parked in front of your house four nights in a row, I figured I'd give the neighbors something else to talk about."

She pushed it closed and locked it. "Do you think they're counting?"

His grin unleashed both dimples. "Absolutely. But I remind myself—"

"They mean well." They finished his sentence together, ending in a laugh.

"How is Mary Jo? I haven't spoken to her today."

He wrapped an arm across her shoulder and walked her through the dining room to the kitchen. "She's good. She asked me to tell you Thanksgiving dinner will be at six."

"Are you going to be able to make it?"

He nodded. "Since I'm off that day, I was planning to head to Corsicana in the morning and hang out with my family, then be back in time for dinner at Mary Jo's." Facing her, he linked their hands. "I'd like you to come home with me."

She shook her head. "Oh, no. It's a holiday. I don't want to intrude on your family time."

"Trust me. They're way more interested in meeting you than seeing me. In fact, my mom offered to call you with an invitation if it would make you feel better."

"You told her about me?"

The look he gave her suggested he couldn't believe she would ask such a ridiculous question. "Riley, I talk about you to anyone who'll listen."

How could she let a romantic line like that go unrewarded? With a sigh, she rose onto her toes, slid her arms around his neck, and captured his mouth in a kiss. Sam's arms banded around her as he deepened it.

When she felt herself spiraling into that blissful place of stirring desire, she fitted her palms to his broad chest and pushed back. Another sigh. "However delightful, this is not the way to get dinner on the table."

He leaned in for a last, smacking kiss. "I'm only agreeing because I'm starving." He gestured toward the back door. "You want me to feed the dogs?"

"I'd appreciate it. And I'll call you when it's time to sit down."

She knew the second the puppies realized he was outside by the wild, excited barking. They were as crazy about him as she was.

She thought about Thanksgiving as she pulled the green salad she'd made earlier from the refrigerator. Meeting his family sounded like a big step, especially since they specifically requested her presence.

The invitation was equal parts flattering and scary. The opinion of his family mattered to Sam, making it doubly important they like her. At least she was confident she had his older sister's vote. As many times as she'd taken the puppies to the clinic, she and Sherry had developed a fun, fledgling friendship.

The timer pinged. She walked the salad to the table, pulled on a pair of pot holders and slid the casserole from the oven. When she heard a knock on the front door, she set it on the stove to cool.

Riley was mentally going through the contents of her closet as she slipped off the pot holders and laid them on the dining room table. She'd pretty much decided a casual dress would make the best impression on Sam's family, neat without trying too hard, when she unlocked the door and swung it open.

She sucked in a breath.

Ron Pearson, the man of her nightmares, loomed just inches away.

Shock and horror immobilized her.

He'd found her.

A split second later her survival instincts kicked in, and she slammed the wood panel. Too late. He stopped it with his palm, pushed it wide.

Her stalker walked into her home like a welcome visitor.

"You seem surprised to see me." He sent her a self-satisfied smile as he closed the door. The cold look in his eyes chilled her to her bones.

"What—" Terror set off every alarm inside her, and she began to shake. "How did you find me?"

She hated the tremors in her body, in her voice. She'd let him bully her once. She hated that she was allowing him to do it again.

"Better question, how did you think you could leave me? Baby, we're a team." Her stomach turned as he stroked a possessive hand along her hair. "I've been worried about you. You know we're meant to be together. That I'm crazy about you."

Crazy *being the operative word.*

"I know you've been under a lot of stress since the funeral." He gave her a disapproving wag of his head. "So, I forgive you for worrying me sick with your little disappearance. However, it's clear we'll have to do something to ensure it doesn't happen again." He clenched and unclenched his fists. "I'd be devastated if anything happened to you."

Ron was toying with her, feeding her obvious fear.

Even as her knees knocked together, she got angry. How dare he show up and try to steal the joy she'd found? She'd rolled over once. Let him drive her from her home, her life. No more.

She was finished being a victim.

"After I saw a picture of you posted on the Village Green web-site . . . great costume by the way . . . it was easy . . ."

While he recounted his cleverness in finding her through social media, Riley scanned the area for a weapon. Head bowed as if sub-mitting to his authority, she surreptitiously searched for something, anything, to use against him.

Two oven mitts and a stack of assignments she needed to grade sat on the dining room table. A paper cut wouldn't slow him down, and she couldn't count on him to hold still long enough for her to smother him with the pot holders.

*Help me, Jesus.*

"Okay, guys, back in the kennel." Sam clapped his hands for atten-tion. "You've had your turn getting fed, now it's mine."

Herding puppies was an exercise in futility. He'd get two headed in the direction of the chain-link enclosure when the others would come bounding up and chase them in the opposite direction. If he tried to bend over to grab them, they would hunker down until the last possible second then sprint away.

Shadow waited patiently at the back door for him to finish his little game so they could go inside.

"You could help me, you know."

The dog flopped down on her stomach. The way her tongue lolled out, it looked like she was laughing at him.

It took a good five minutes to corral the black-and-white terrors. As the last one ran into the kennel, he set the latch and blew out a breath. "Time for you to be adopted so someone else can chase you."

Last he heard, Riley had families for three of them. No way she could keep them, but he knew she dreaded the moment when she had to let the beloved puppies go.

Halfway to the house, he stopped. Shadow was on her feet and facing the back door. Her hackles were up, and her head tilted as though she was listening to something inside. She gave a low, guttural growl.

"What's up, girl?"

She glanced over her shoulder at him before scratching at the door.

His first thought, that Riley was hurt, propelled him to the dog's side at a dead run. But something about the dog's deep-throated growl stopped him from bursting in. If Riley was injured, Shadow would sound worried, not fierce.

All senses on alert, he reached for his gun before remembering he wasn't in uniform. *Great.* He was unarmed. Keeping low in case anyone watched from the house, he dashed into the garage, looking for a weapon. Since he couldn't very well enter swinging a shovel or rake, he settled for a package of zip ties. In less than a minute, he eased open the back door and, finding no one in the kitchen, slipped inside.

"I'm so surprised to see you, Ron." Riley's voice, unnaturally loud, came from the front of the house. "I hadn't expected you to travel here from Oklahoma City."

Good girl. Nice job feeding him information.

Sam reached behind him and closed the door with a solid click. "Hey, Riley," he called. "You in here?"

Her long pause indicated she hadn't expected him to announce his presence. "Yes. In the front hall."

Shadow at his side, he ambled through the kitchen and dining room as though adrenaline wasn't pushing through his body and his heart wasn't pounding through his chest. He stopped several feet from Riley and the guy he recognized from her description as the stalker and adopted a look of happy surprise. "Oh, hey, I didn't know you had company."

"Who are you?" Ron demanded.

"He's a neighbor." Riley's hands were locked in front of her in a white-knuckled grip, and her voice wobbled with strain.

Sam closed the distance and stretched out a hand in introduction. "Sam Walker."

Ron ignored it. "Take off. Riley and I are having an important conversation." His harsh tone earned a growl from Shadow.

"Who are you?" Sam kept his tone light, expression friendly as he analyzed the situation. Though agitated, Ron didn't appear to pose an immediate threat. No sign of a gun or knife.

Cold, dark eyes locked onto his. "I'm her boyfriend, if it's any business of yours."

Sam's smile never faltered. "Since she's dating me, I guess I'm gonna to have to make it my business." He turned to Riley. "Why don't you finish whatever you were doing while your friend and I figure this out."

Ron's arm snaked out to grab her as she tried to move away. Eyes wide with fear, she gasped as he hauled her up tight against him. Shadow barked and circled their feet.

This time the growl was Sam's. "You're going to want to let go of the lady."

"You're going to want to shut your mouth. And call off your stupid dog, before I hurt both of you."

"I really don't think you want to be threatening me." To avoid escalating the situation, Sam kept his body language casual as he held his position. "This is probably a good time to mention I'm a police officer."

Ron glared. "It's not a threat, idiot. It's a promise. And I don't care who you are. Get out."

Riley watched the exchange between them in silence. Suddenly, she sagged in Ron's arms, stomped his instep with the heel of her shoe, drove her elbow into his stomach, and rotated out of his hold—all in one quick, seamless move.

Sam was so impressed with her textbook execution self-defense move that he made the rookie mistake of taking his eyes off the perp. Ron swung and connected hard with Sam's jaw.

"Go," Sam shouted to Riley as he delivered a punishing hit to Ron's chin and a quick follow-up blow to his gut.

She bolted from the room.

Like most bullies, Ron wasn't much of a fighter when matched with someone his size. Another couple of punches, and a lucky fall over Shadow who tangled herself in his feet, and Ron sprawled on the floor.

The zip ties came in handy for binding his hands and feet. Sam left Shadow standing guard with the instructions, "If he moves, bite him."

Riley stood in the dining room, shell-shocked look in her eyes, cell phone in her hand. "I called the police. They're on their way."

He closed the distance between them and opened his arms. She stepped in. For a long moment he just held her, feeling the reassuring beat of her heart against his. At last, when both were calmer, he took a step back to cradle her face in his hands. He kept his voice low to prevent Ron from overhearing him. "You okay?"

She nodded. "Your poor face. He hit you hard."

His jaw throbbed, and he knew he'd be sporting a shiner. "Lucky shot. I was so busy watching you do your Wonder Woman thing, I left myself open. You nailed it. Or should I say him?"

She gave him a wobbly smile. "I guess I can admit now that while I didn't think practicing self-defense moves was such a great way to spend our dates, I'm very glad we did."

He stroked a thumb across her cheek. "I'm so sorry you had to use them."

Tears welled in her eyes. "It's okay. It's over. You saved me."

He leaned in and kissed her forehead. "Nope, I can't take credit for that. You saved yourself. Once again, I just came in for the cleanup."

Dispatch pulled the captain off the desk and called in one of their part-time officers to handle the arrest. As they led him to the squad car, Ron protested mightily that they didn't have anything on him, that he hadn't done anything wrong. He swore he'd be out in twenty-four hours, and the look he sent Riley said he'd be back.

"*Do* we have anything on him?" she asked as they stood on the porch to watch the car pull away.

"A couple of assault charges." But even with assaulting an officer, they didn't have enough to take this guy out of the picture. "I'm going to follow them to the station. I want to be present and make sure they take a hard look at him."

"Good idea."

Sam opened the door and stood aside for her to enter the house ahead of him. "You need to pack an overnight bag. I'll call Mary Jo and tell her you're coming. You've been through a lot tonight. I don't want you to be alone."

"Okay, Officer Bossy." The fact she didn't argue with him told him just how shaken she was. She headed for the kitchen. "First, I'm going to make an ice pack for your face."

He followed her, stopping by the casserole on the stove while she loaded ice cubes into a plastic sandwich bag, then wrapped it in a dish towel. "Dinner smells delicious." He didn't know what it was about the aftermath of a fight that made him so hungry. "I don't think we should waste it."

"Help yourself." She pressed the ice pack into his hands then turned to leave. "I couldn't eat a thing."

In the way of men everywhere, he ate directly from the baking dish, forking up bites while Riley packed, and he talked to Mary Jo on the phone. When he finished, he covered the pan and put it into the refrigerator, along with the untouched salad.

Riley rejoined him in the kitchen as he rinsed his fork and put it in the dishwasher. "Got everything you need?"

She raised the small duffle she carried. "Yes, but I'm having second thoughts. I'm really fine, and I hate to be an imposition on Mary Jo."

"Are you kidding? She loves slumber parties. She invited Shadow too."

Frowning, she glanced toward the backyard. "What about the puppies?"

"They've been fed and watered for the night. They'll do fine in the kennel."

They drove the short block to Mary Jo's in Riley's SUV. She met them at the door, hugging first Riley, then Sam, then Riley again. "Praise God! I'm so thankful you're both safe."

Sam grinned. "It was pretty intense, but Riley was amazing."

"Of course she was." Her arm still around Riley, Mary Jo bustled them inside. "I have your bath all ready, dear one. Your job is to soak until you're nice and sleepy, then we'll tuck you in for a good rest."

Mary Jo turned to him. "Sam, when you're done with whatever you need to do, why don't you come back here for the night? You can sleep in the other guest room. It'll be comforting to be together, and we can have a nice visit over breakfast."

"I'm probably going to be late."

She shrugged. "No matter. I'll leave everything ready. You have a key. Just let yourself in."

"Thank you, Mary Jo." He pressed a kiss to her wrinkled cheek. "You're the best."

"You're very welcome. Come on, Shadow." The older woman headed toward the kitchen, dog at her heels. "We'll give you two some privacy to say goodbye. Don't make it too long. I don't want Riley's bath to get cold."

His beautiful, brave Riley had begun to droop. He placed his hands on her shoulders. "Be a good girl and do as Mary Jo says. I'll be here when you wake up in the morning, and I'll be able to tell you what I learn tonight." He bent to kiss her. "Sleep well, Wonder Woman."

It was close to two in the morning when he let himself into Mary Jo's house. He was tired, and his face hurt like crazy, but he was well satisfied with the night's work.

Bless Mary Jo for leaving on the hall light so he could see to make his way to the stairs. He slipped off his shoes and climbed to the second floor without making a sound. He left his duffle outside the bedroom he used when he stayed at Mary Jo's and continued down the hall.

Quietly, so as not to disturb her, he eased open the door of the other guest room and peeked inside. The night light in the adjoining bathroom gave enough illumination for him to see Riley asleep in the four-poster bed. Shadow lifted her head and thumped her tail as she lay on the floor beside her. He stood there for a moment, content to listen to Riley's slow, rhythmic breathing and to know the woman he loved was safe.

Powerful emotions expanded in his chest. He loved her.

He'd been falling for her so long, probably since the day he showed up at her door with poor Shadow. He admired her then for her compassion and spirit. As he got to know her better, he admired her more. Riley was the perfect combination of beauty, brains, and heart. The kind of person who made the world a better place wherever she went.

The long-awaited answer to his prayers.

*Thank you, God. For bringing us together. And for keeping her safe. Thank you for your faithfulness.*

With one last look, he moved back into the hall and pulled her door closed. He loved her. No doubt about it. He wanted to tell her. Heck, he wanted to tell everyone.

But the timing wasn't right.

The last few months had been rough for her. Losing her dad, being stalked by a nutcase, and starting all over in a new place— here was a woman who needed some time to process and heal.

He'd give her time. *Not too long.* He trusted that the same God who brought her to him would show him when the moment was right to declare his love and ask for hers.

By the time he showered and dressed the next morning, the ladies were already downstairs enjoying breakfast and a cup of coffee at the kitchen table. As he entered the kitchen, he homed in on Riley. She looked relaxed, well-rested. With her hair up in a ponytail and her freshly scrubbed face, she had that wholesome cheerleader thing going on he'd noticed the first time he met her.

She looked up when he walked in and hit him with a smile so warm, he felt it down to his toes. "Good morning."

Man, he loved that woman. "Good morning, yourself."

Mary Jo stood. "Let me fix you a cup of coffee, Sam."

He waved her back into her seat. "I've got it." As familiar with her home as his own, he pulled a mug from the cabinet by the sink and filled it from the pot on the counter. "How'd everyone sleep last night?"

"Amazingly well."

He carried his coffee to the table and sat in the chair next to Riley. "I've got some news that will ensure many more peaceful nights."

Riley put down her fork. "You found something on Ron."

He nodded. "Ron, aka Roland Purcell, has been a very busy man. We ran his prints and found all kinds of open cases waiting for him to surface. Swindling lone females seems to be his crime of choice, but he's dabbled in assault and burglary as well. I think it's safe to say there are enough charges to lock him away for a lifetime."

"Will Riley have to testify against him?" Mary Jo asked.

"Possibly. Honestly, the charges we brought against him are insignificant compared to the others. We'll file everything we have, but it won't be Riley who sends him away."

"So, you were right about him. That he targeted me for my inheritance."

Sam nodded. "He didn't admit it, but based on his history, it looks that way."

Mary Jo beamed at them. "You two make a wonderful team."

He reached over to take Riley's hand. "The best."

# CHAPTER THIRTEEN

The next month passed quickly, with anticipation for Christmas consuming the entire town. Decorations brightened the downtown area and surrounded the Green. Now, in the week before Christmas, Riley's classroom had taken on a new energy. With Sam expected for one more reading before the holiday, Riley used the free time before her class returned from recess to update her December bulletin boards. Shadow's board had four new pictures. As each family came to claim their puppy, she'd snapped a shot of them holding the dog to display in the classroom.

Under Pink's picture, she hung a smiling photo of Trey and Hallie, with the dog in Hallie's lap. Under Red, she attached one of Joe, Eden, and Jake carefully holding their new puppy. Chris and his mother cradled their new pet in Green's picture. The last photograph was her very favorite—a shot of Blue licking Mrs. Cooper's face while Mr. Cooper looked on.

Almost from the beginning she'd known who wanted the first three puppies, but Blue's fate had remained a mystery. To exercise some control over who adopted them, she hadn't done any advertising. When word of mouth didn't bring a family for Blue, she wondered if she'd be keeping him. She'd mentioned the situation to the Coopers during one of their FaceTime visits before Thanksgiving and was stunned when they said they wanted to adopt the dog.

Mr. Cooper explained that following Shadow's story from the beginning had been a highlight for them during his wife's cancer treatments. The laughs they got from watching the puppies had been therapeutic for both. He said they'd talked it over and decided that if any of the puppies weren't claimed, they would adopt it.

The Saturday after Thanksgiving, they'd driven up from Houston to collect him. It felt odd to welcome the Coopers into their own home, but Sam had been there to perform the introductions, and the friendship they'd begun through cards and phone calls blossomed. They enjoyed lunch and a great visit before the Coopers loaded into their car and headed home, their new puppy cradled in Mrs. Cooper's arms.

Twenty rosy-cheeked children flooded into the classroom as she finished attaching the last picture.

"Okay, hang up your coats and get back to your seats. Officer Sam will be here soon to read to us."

Their bubbling excitement mirrored her own. Just being in the same room with him lit her up like the Christmas tree he'd helped her set out in her living room a week ago.

Sam knocked on the doorframe and poked his head into the classroom. Riley stood at the front, writing something on the board. Dressed in slim black slacks and a pretty green sweater the color of her eyes, she was the most beautiful woman he'd ever seen. He could be content to stand there for hours watching her.

She turned and sent him a warm smile. "Hi, Officer Sam. Come in. We've been looking forward to your visit."

The kids greeted him with their usual boisterous enthusiasm. Honestly, there just wasn't anything cuter than first graders.

Book tucked under his arm, he strode to the center front of the room and faced the class. "One more week of school before Christmas break. Anybody ask Santa for something really cool?"

That got them going. It didn't take him long to realize it wasn't working for them all to speak at once. He lifted a hand for silence. "Let's go around the room, and everyone tell us one special thing on your list."

He listened as they each took a turn. Bicycles, scooters, and video games seemed to be the most popular items. Chris cheerfully announced he'd already received his gift, a dog of his own. Knowing that finances remained tight at his house while Darcie waited tables and looked for a better paying job, Sam had dropped off a wrapped video game system from Santa for him to open on Christmas.

"What is Santa bringing you, Officer Sam?"

He pressed his lips together as he considered the question. Socks, no doubt. Probably a new wallet or belt. His sisters usually gave him some fancy-smelling aftershave.

It all sounded fine, but what he really wanted wasn't Santa's to give. He glanced at Riley who scooted a chair over for him to sit on.

All he really wanted for Christmas was her.

He chafed against his commitment to take their relationship slowly. He knew beyond a shadow of a doubt she was *the* one, and he was pretty certain she felt the same way about him. But he also knew she'd been through a lot of emotional turmoil and deserved time to heal before he pressed her on their relationship.

Ron had told Riley he loved her to get his hands on her money. Sam wanted to wait long enough that the taint of Ron's attempted larceny was forgotten before he told Riley he loved her.

He was tired of waiting. Time to test the waters.

"I'm not sure what Santa's got in mind for me." He lowered into the chair. "I guess I'll just have to wait and see. I do know I have a great book to share with you today."

They quieted with gratifying haste.

Suddenly nervous, he cleared his throat. A lot was riding on this particular story. He cleared it again, shifted in his chair, and lifted the book cover to the class so they could see it. "The title of my book today is *How Do You Say I Love You?* by Lauren Haden."

Holding the book high, his fingers trembled as he opened to the first page and read, "Dogs say I love you with a lick of their tongue and a wag of their tail."

After a slow pass to be certain everyone saw the illustrations, he turned the page. "Cats say I love you with a rumbly purr."

Each illustration described how a different animal expressed affection. Finally, he flipped to the last page. "People say I love you with their words. I love you. The end."

Olivia's hand shot into the air. "I love you, Officer Sam."

His heart broke a little at the absolute sweetness of her declaration. "Thank you. I love you too." His gaze swept the room. "All of you."

Olivia's expression turned sly. "Do you love Miss Vreeland?"

Uh-oh. Major tactical error. He walked right into that one. When he decided to test the waters, he'd imagined dipping a toe, not diving in. He'd expected Riley to pick up on the message, not the entire class. He squirmed in his seat as he racked his brain for an acceptable reply to diffuse the awkward situation.

Riley walked to his side and tilted her head expectantly. "Well?"

The fact she sounded neither embarrassed nor offended clarified his next move. He stood and looked into her eyes. "Actually, I love her best."

"I knew it!" Noah pumped his fist.

"Miss Vreeland, do you love Officer Sam?"

The room fell silent as all eyes landed on her.

Gaze locked on his, she nodded. "I do love him. With all my heart."

"My mom says you should marry her." Justin directed his remark to Sam.

Several students nodded sagely.

"It makes sense since you love her."

*Whoa!* When he lost control of a situation, he did it in a big way. Sam shook his head. "It's not that simple. I have to ask her first." *In private.*

"You can ask her now," Olivia said. She folded her hands on top of her desk. "We'll wait."

Oh man. This was not the way he planned it. After asking God for a nudge when the timing was right, he'd expected candlelight and soft music. It never crossed his mind he'd be declaring his love in front of an audience of eager first graders.

Still. He was here and she was here. And he was tired of waiting. He took Riley's hand and looked into her eyes. "Ms. Vreeland, would you do me the very great honor of becoming my wife?"

"That means he wants to marry you."

Riley smiled and nodded. "Yes, Officer Sam. I would be happy to marry you and become your wife."

The room erupted in applause.

"You should probably kiss her now," Olivia instructed. "That's what they do in movies."

Gagging sounds came from the back of the room.

Riley shook her head as she squeezed his hand before releasing it. "Maybe in movies, but not first-grade classrooms. Everyone say goodbye to Officer Sam, then go ahead and finish the math papers we started before recess."

They converged on him in a noisy huddle. After he'd hugged and acknowledged each one, he caught Riley's eye and motioned toward the door with his head.

"Time to take out your work." She waited until they were settled before meeting him just outside the door.

He searched her face, looking for what she really thought about his crazy proposal. "I'm sorry. Really. I don't know what to say—"

She smiled. "You ask me if I liked your story."

The smile was a good sign. "Did you?"

Eyes on his, she nodded. "Best one yet."

He lowered his voice. "I didn't mean for it to go down like it did, but I meant every word I said back there. I love you, Riley. And I want to marry you."

"I sure hope so, since I have twenty witnesses."

He had to laugh. "When I pictured popping the question, I envisioned someplace quiet and romantic."

Her eyes danced. "What could be more romantic than getting prompts and tips from a class of six- and seven-year-olds?"

His worries vanished. He should have known Riley would see the humor in it. "I don't know about romantic, but it was definitely memorable. Something to tell our grandkids."

"I have only one complaint."

"After that fiasco, I'm surprised it's only one."

"It doesn't feel official until I get my kiss."

His gaze lowered to her very kissable mouth. "I'm not too happy about that part either. Tell you what. Meet me after school and we'll seal the deal."

She grinned. "It's a date."

"I love you, Ms. Vreeland."

"I love you, too, Officer Sam."

Mrs. Peeper stood outside the administrative offices as he was leaving the school. She smiled. "Hello, Officer Sam. How was story time today?"

"Eventful." He stopped. He couldn't very well breeze past her without some sort of explanation since she was bound to hear about it. He cleared his throat. "I just proposed to Ms. Vreeland in front of her class."

Mrs. Peeper's mouth opened then closed without a sound. The unflappable principal seemed at a loss for words. She gave it another try. "That seems rather . . . public."

"Yes ma'am. And I'm sorry. If you get any calls from parents . . ." *What could he possibly offer as damage control?* "Tell them we'll invite them to the wedding."

# EPILOGUE

Sam stood with Pastor Dale in the front center aisle. Sam's dad and Trey and Joe stood at his side as groomsmen.

The pre-ceremony noise in the sanctuary was especially loud, not surprising since a significant portion of the bride's side of the church was comprised of recently graduated first graders and their families. Dressed in their Sunday best, all twenty of Riley's students were seated in rows just behind Mary Jo and the Coopers in the family pew.

Sam fidgeted, tugging at his collar.

"Nervous?" Pastor Dale whispered.

Sam shook his head. "Just ready. I've been waiting for her for a long time."

The organist began the music signaling the bridesmaids' entry.

Hallie came first, Eden followed, and behind her was Kathleen, Riley's maid of honor and childhood friend from Oklahoma. The three ladies in their long pink dresses with matching bouquets took their places on the opposite side of the aisle.

Sam's heart beat double time as the music changed and the congregation stood in anticipation of his bride's entry. The doors leading into the sanctuary swung open, revealing the answer to his prayers and the desire of his heart.

*Thank you, God.*

208 208   The Perfect Getaway

Always beautiful, Riley was stunning in a pure white dress and veil. Tears filled his eyes as she slowly made her way down the aisle toward him.

"Breathe, buddy," Joe whispered.

When she was still several feet away, Sam couldn't wait any longer. He broke protocol and stepped toward her, extending his hand. Her brows lifted, probably at the unscripted move, but the wide smile on her face as she took it told him she understood his impatience.

Interlacing their fingers, he lifted her hand and kissed it before turning to face the altar.

Riley wished her parents could be here. She hoped they shared in the day, peeking down from heaven to see the picture-perfect ceremony. She wanted them to hear Pastor Dale's wise words and know the bone-deep love and security she found in her soon-to-be husband.

A handsome man in uniform or faded jeans and ratty T-shirt, Sam was magnificent in a tuxedo. Strong and self-assured, yet gentle and compassionate, he was everything she could ask for and more.

As they spoke their vows, a deeply intimate moment in spite of a full sanctuary of onlookers, she was confident her heart and future were safe with this man.

At last, Pastor Dale declared them man and wife. "Sam, you may kiss your bride."

"Ewww." The groaned protest came from somewhere in the first-grade contingent.

The congregation chuckled good-naturedly while Riley leaned in to kiss her groom. It was difficult to engage in a proper kiss when both parties were laughing, so she settled for a quick smooch and the promise of a lifetime of kisses.